TERI BARNETT

Cupcakes ARE MURDER

BIJOUX MYSTERY SERIES: BOOK 3

LUCKY CROW PRESS

Cupcakes are Murder
Bijoux Mystery Series: Book 3
Published Internationally by Teri Barnett
USA
Copyright © 2021 Teri Barnett
teribarnett.com
Lucky Crow Press

Exclusive cover © 2021 Mystery Cover Designs
Interior design © 2021 Indie Book Designer

PRINT ISBN 978-1-7365413-3-3
EBOOK ISBN 978-1-7365413-2-6

Editor: Joanna D'Angelo

For Hannah

ACKNOWLEDGMENTS

As always, a huge thank you to Indiana Writers' Workshop for their critiques and encouragement and especially to my beta readers from the group: Tony Perona, Jeff Stanger, and June Clair (all fabulous authors!)

And thank you, too, to Joanna D'Angelo, an amazing editor, great cheerleader, and friend.

CONTENTS

CHAPTER 1

"Officer down."

The call every cop dreads hearing.

Morgan Hart rushed to the address given over the car radio, her heart in her throat. She'd been out on a lunch run for her and her partner, Liz Shore. A wave of panic washed over Morgan as she turned onto the street. She had no explanation for it, but it took her breath away. Pulling up to the location, she saw her husband Ian's truck parked at the curb.

Maybe Ian was in the area? Maybe he heard the same call I did. Maybe he got here just before me….

But the anxiety, now laced with fear, grew and intensified when she locked eyes with Liz. Her partner of five years and dear friend rushed to stop her from going into the alley. James Wheat, Ian's partner, blocked Morgan after she pushed past Liz.

"You don't want to see this," James whispered harshly.

Morgan shoved him aside and ran down the alley. She stopped and froze, staring down at the sheet-draped body, a pool of blood soaked the ground around it.

Morgan looked up at Rosanna Jensen, the medical examiner. Her eyes pleaded with the older woman. *Please!* The word was lodged in her throat.

Rosanna nodded and pulled the sheet back.

Single gunshot wound to the chest.

He would've died instantly, felt nothing.

Morgan crumpled to the ground, feeling everything.

"Ian!" she screamed.

I'm here. The strong arms enveloped her, held her tight.

"Don't leave me," Morgan murmured, wrapping her arms around him.

I'm sorry….

"No. Please."

I have to go. You can't live in the past, Fay. You have to unlock it and let it go. I love you…

"Don't leave—" Morgan's eyes flew open, her arms tightly gripping her pillow, her legs tangled in the sheets. Ian was the only one who ever called her by her middle name, *Fay*. She sat upright, disoriented. Looked around her bedroom, her eye caught the clock. 3 a.m. She shoved her choppy brunette hair out of her eyes.

So real. So close.

Griselda, her black cat, was sitting at the foot of the bed, watching her.

"C'mere Gris," Morgan patted her leg and the large feline climbed into her lap. Morgan had adopted the Maine Coon after the cat's fortune-telling owner was murdered a couple of months ago. Gris placed a paw on her hand and began purring. Morgan took a steadying breath, cradled Gris close, and lay back down. A single tear ran down her cheek.

"How am I supposed to let him go when his murderer is still out there?" Morgan whispered into the cat's soft fur.

Gris mewed.

Morgan sighed and settled back under the covers of her bed in the cozy beachside cottage she inherited from her late mom, Billie. Gris curled up tighter beside her.

I came back to Bijoux to get away from a stressful and complicated life and now it feels like I've gone and stepped into another one.

Her return to her hometown was supposed to be easy, a fresh start, a small town with a slower pace. And a chance for Morgan to untangle her life from her past as a homicide detective in Detroit. And more importantly, a way to try to let go of the pain of Ian's murder and her mom, Billie's, death from colon cancer a few years ago.

At Able's encouragement, Morgan moved back to Bijoux to take on the job of police captain, a job her dad had held for thirty-plus years. "Nothing ever happens in Bijoux," he told her. "You know that kiddo."

Morgan had had a strained relationship with her dad over the years, after her parents divorced when Morgan was just fourteen. Her move back home was supposed to be a new beginning for the two of them as well.

She was pleasantly surprised to find Able had moved on after his split with Billie and he'd found love again and married Zoe Buffet. Together, the two of them took over Hal's Hardware Store, turning it into one of the main gathering places in Bijoux.

Then, on her first day on the job, a murder. Three more followed over the summer. The first ones Bijoux had seen in almost a hundred years and they were happening on her watch.

Unacceptable.

Dreams. Nightmares. They were all the same, whether she slept or didn't sleep. She was increasingly tired. Exhausted. Most nights spent tossing and turning, intent on solving the cases in front of her. Intent on solving Ian's murder from five years ago. Her husband had been working undercover. The investigative officers declared it a drug deal gone bad.

Morgan had other ideas.

"I will not let go, Ian," she whispered as her eyelids grew heavy once more. "Not until I find your killer."

"Whoa, Cap'n," JJ said as Morgan walked into the station. It was Thursday morning and Jeremy Jones, aka JJ, the solid, five-foot-ten, red-headed deputy was leaning against the worn oak front counter, talking to his girlfriend, Hannah Bellamy of Hannah's Heavenly Confections. Hannah was also a red head but almost a foot shorter and a lot curvier.

"What?" Morgan's eyes narrowed, daring him to speak.

JJ held up his hands. "Nothing. You just look like you've been wrestling Griselda." He grimaced. "And Gris won."

Morgan took a sip from the to-go cup of rich, black coffee she'd picked up at Dave's Deli on the way to work. Jerome, the ever opinionated waiter, had commented about her appearance, too, only he went

3

into great detail about the puffiness around her eyes and possible remedies.

"What you look like is you could use one of these." Hannah opened the magenta and green polka-dotted box sitting on the counter and lifted out a cupcake. "Triple Mochaccino." She smiled as she handed the work of culinary art to Morgan. "Dark chocolate cake, whipped milk chocolate frosting, coffee crème center. And vanilla sprinkles."

"Oh, my goodness. I've already had breakfast, but I can definitely make room for one of these." Morgan closed her eyes and all but purred as she inhaled the aroma of rich chocolate and coffee in her hand. She peeled back a bit of the delicate turquoise paper and took a bite of cake and frosting. Just the perfect amount of each. "Hannah, would you like to be my new deputy?" Morgan looked over at JJ. "There's going to be an opening for that position very soon." She took another small bite. "You will, of course, have to bring these in every day."

Hannah laughed. "Thanks, but I have my hands full with the bakery."

"Seriously, Cap'n," JJ said. "Are you all right? Because you don't look all right."

Morgan paused mid-bite and stared at him over the top of the cupcake. "Do you have a death wish today?"

"Who has a death wish?" Caleb Joseph asked as he strolled into the station. The six-foot two, dark-haired owner of The Raven's Nest Bookstore, former U of M English lit professor, and best-selling, gothic romance writer (under a *nom de plume*), flashed a grin. "And should I be worried?"

"It's not always about you, Cal." Morgan glanced over at him, noticed he was wearing faded jeans that molded to his lean legs and a red-plaid flannel shirt today, the sleeves rolled to his elbows. *Interesting.* Cal never dressed down.

Cal glanced back, then stopped and looked her up and down. "Damn, Morgan. I know it's been challenging with those murder cases since you got here, but you probably should try to look, well...."

She scowled at him. "Look like what, exactly?"

"Less like the cat won?" he offered.

4

"That's exactly what I said!" JJ grinned.

"What is wrong with you people?" Morgan looked down at herself. Okay, maybe her blue and khaki uniform wasn't as freshly pressed as usual, and maybe she'd neglected to use the lint brush this morning after giving Gris a cuddle before she left, and maybe her sleep was riddled with nightmares lately. But that didn't mean anything. She sighed, tucked a wayward strand of hair behind an ear and picked a fluff of cat fur off her pant leg. "I'm fine. Why do you guys insist on getting into my business? I promise, I'll tell you if I need help."

"No, you won't," Cal countered. "That's not who you are, Captain Morgan."

Morgan shrugged and took another bite of the cupcake. *There. Cupcakes make everything better.*

"You're eating it wrong," Cal said.

Morgan's brows lifted. "I beg your pardon?"

"Everyone knows you eat a cupcake from the bottom up. Save the frosting and sprinkles for last." Cal looked at Hannah. "Am I mistaken?"

Hannah shook her head. "I am not getting in the middle of this argument. Been there, done that."

"JJ?"

"Actually, you'd be wrong there, Cal." JJ picked up a cupcake with vanilla Swiss meringue frosting and silver sprinkles. It looked like a mini-wedding cake. "Being the stuffy professor you are, I can see why you'd think starting with the cake is better, since that's boring. The truth is, you dive headfirst into the icing, then top it off with the cake and a glass of ice cold milk." He took a giant bite, leaving frosting on both sides of his mouth. Hannah giggled and handed him a napkin.

"You're both ridiculous," Morgan interjected. "You eat them simul-taneously. That way you get the best of both worlds, at the same time." She shook her head. "I don't know what's wrong with you two. And I mean that on a lot of levels."

"Well, you'll soon have the opportunity to ask the cupcake queen herself the best way to eat one of these," Cal said, holding up his caramel drizzled milk chocolate cupcake with whipped cherry butter-cream frosting.

"Hannah has already refused to participate in this discussion," Morgan said around another bite, washing it down with a sip of coffee.

Hannah laughed. "While I appreciate you think I'm the queen, there's only one true cupcake queen and that'd be Sassy McComas. Her fans call her Queen Sass. And she's the founder of Queenie's Loquacious Cakes. She's from the UK but made her baking name here in the States on the Baking Network." Hannah clapped her hands together. "She's my idol. I still can't believe she's bringing her Baker's Dozen Hometown Cupcake Bake-off right here to Bijoux!"

"That's this week already?" Morgan asked. It wasn't like her to forget something as important as an event that could bring hundreds of outsiders to Bijoux. Potential trouble for her small town, especially since Cal was organizing it and murder seemed to happen at every event he touched. First it was the romance writers' conference, then the psychic fair. And with the highly anticipated contest coming up, Morgan was worried about a killer triple hat trick.

I need to get myself together. She glanced at Cal, saw the worry in his eyes, and decided to ignore it.

"You do remember Hannah and I entered Bijoux in the Baker's Dozen Bake-off for a chance to host the competition, right?" Cal asked. "And we won."

"Of course, I do," Morgan replied. "Tell me, does that have anything to do with why you're dressed like a lumberjack?"

"Ah, deflecting. This I can deal with. Yes, it's why I'm *casually* dressed. The Raven's Nest is, of course, Bijoux's main sponsor of the event. Plus, I'm helping to get things set up at the community center. We've enlisted some of the art students from the high school, too. They're painting a mural of giant confections on one side of the building. Dancing cakes and things." He paused. "No porn star mustaches, though. I was pretty clear that was a no-go."

Morgan snorted. Her first day back in Bijoux, besides dealing with the murder of a famous romance writer, found her and JJ investigating a graffiti 'artist' who was going around painting giant Tom Selleck-esque mustaches on everything.

"And you thought you'd dress like them?" JJ interjected. "Dude, you look like one of the Village People."

Cal carefully placed his cupcake on the counter, stepped to the center of the space, did a spin and then spelled out the Y M C A letters with his arms. He gave a slight bow as Hannah clapped and hooted, then walked back over and continued eating his cupcake. From the bottom up.

JJ whistled. "I did not see that coming."

"No one did, JJ." Morgan just stared at Cal. "No one did." She shook her head. "Wow. So, other than entertaining us with your dance moves, why are you here, anyway? Need to report that squirrel who keeps emptying your bird feeder?"

"That squirrel does need a citation, but that's not why I'm here." Cal popped the rest of the cupcake in his mouth and grinned. "I'm heading over to the community center. Thought you might like to tag along."

Morgan walked around the counter and plopped down onto her desk chair. Pulling a lint roller out of a drawer she began to clean the cat fur from her uniform. "Why would I want to do that?"

"Don't you want to scope out potential evil-doers?" Cal frowned. "Seriously. This is not like you, Morgan."

Morgan sighed. Cal was right. Not that she'd tell him that. She pushed away from her desk, slipped on her silver aviator sunglasses, and said, "All right. Let's go. But I'm not tagging along. I'm driving."

CHAPTER 2

MORGAN AND CAL got into the police Ford Ranger and drove east on Main Street, away from Lake Michigan. Morgan couldn't help noticing that several of the "Hold-Outs"—those who'd initially resisted modernizing the outside of their businesses in order to hang onto that old-school lakeside charm—had begun gentrification makeovers. "Looks like Mayor Ed is getting to more people," Morgan said. Ed Peltier, Bijoux's current mayor, was on a mission to 'clean up' the town and get all shop owners to comply with a beautification order he'd implemented.

Cal shook his head. "Ed's been busy with his threats of imposed fines. Some of the merchants are starting to take him seriously."

"What about you? Are you going to renovate the Raven's Nest?" Morgan couldn't begin to imagine the old bookstore looking different from what it had always looked like. The old shiplap siding had lost most of its paint over the years and was weathered to a soft gray. The large wrap-around porch on the two-story structure had just the right amount of lean to make a child feel like they might slide on it in the winter (she knew this from experience). And the black wrought iron fence surrounding the property was faded and rusting in spots. She'd spent a lot of time there as a child, hanging out with Cal's uncle, Baptiste St. Aubien, a grizzled old man with a soft heart. Cal inherited the shop when Baptiste passed away several years ago.

Cal shrugged. "I have a lot of plans for the store, but an exterior renovation isn't part of them. At this point, anyway. I happen to like how it looks."

"Probably for the best. Knowing you, you'd likely pick out some hideous color that would keep people away. Puce, maybe."

"Please, I have better taste than that."

"As evidenced by your lumberjack-ness today." Morgan grinned as she turned the truck south on Apple Street, toward the Bijoux Community Center. The center was housed in a 1960s brick-and-block building that had once served as a local grade school. When Bijoux, its sister town Lac Voo, and neighboring Grand Pere (a trio of towns jokingly referred to as the "Bermuda Triangle" of Odawa County by the locals because of strange happenings over the years) voted to consolidate their school districts in the early 2010s, the old building was abandoned. Luckily, the town council saw it as a great opportunity to bring folks together and provide a space for classes and activities, so it wasn't vacant for long.

Morgan slowed the truck to a crawl. "That's a lot of action," she commented. The street was lined with cars and people were bustling in and out of the center, hauling equipment, baking supplies, and props.

Cal angled his head out the passenger window and scanned the activity. "About what you'd expect for a large production like this."

Morgan laughed. "And you've been involved in a lot of these sorts of things, have you? Big productions?"

"I'll have you know I had my own show back in the day on the University of Michigan local channel. I read from the classics." He smiled. "I wore a silk jacket and sipped tea. It was all very proper. Well, until I introduced Edgar Allan Poe." The smile became a frown. "Once I started reading his mysteries, complaints started rolling in. Seems most folks wanted more Mr. Darcy and less murderous ape."

She looked at him out of the corner of her eye while still trying to find a parking spot. "Go figure."

"There's a spot opening up over there." He pointed down the street about half a block. "They didn't realize what they had until I quit the show. I made those stories come to life."

Morgan pulled into the spot and shut off the truck. She turned to Cal. "I'm sure you did. Probably like your Y M C A presentation. Which I hope to never see again." She got out and pocketed the keys. "Now let's make sure everyone here stays alive this weekend, okay? Lately, your events are more dangerous than being upside down in a roller coaster with no seatbelts."

He exited the truck and closed the door. "I promise you I've had many events with no bodies. This year has been an unfortunate fluke. Not to mention there are many folks who connect your arrival in Bijoux with breaking our hundred-year streak of no murders."

She shot him a frown. "You sound like our not-so-dear news reporter, Connie Graham." Connie was Morgan's ongoing nightmare— a conspiracy theorist with a microphone who blamed Morgan's return for everything bad that happened in Bijoux. Connie was also Morgan's former childhood best-friend-turned nemesis. Morgan pushed thoughts of Connie away, preferring not to focus too closely on her childhood. There were happy times when she was growing up, for sure, but also more painful memories than she could count—mostly of her parents arguments and divorce and her mother's cancer that still twisted in her gut.

"To paraphrase an old proverb, say enough things and, at some point, you'll get at least one of them right."

"What *old proverb* is that?" Morgan strode to the double glass and aluminum entry doors and pulled one open for a crew member who had her hands full of stage lights. "You know what? Never mind. I don't want to know. I don't want to think about Connie. Let's just go inside and look around."

Cal opened the other door and bowed with a flourish. "As you wish."

Morgan's stomach flipped. *Dammit.* Did he know *The Princess Bride* was one of her favorite movies? She checked her memory. Had she let that slip? It didn't matter. *Ignore him*, she thought, as she walked into the center and stopped just inside the door. People continued to bustle around her, in and out, but she didn't see them. She was twelve years old again.

Cal walked up. "Old memories?"

"You could say that. I went to school here before Mom and Dad divorced and Mom moved us to Detroit." Morgan scanned the long hallway ahead of them, noticed the front office had been converted into a conference room and the old vinyl tile floor had been removed and the concrete beneath it was now sealed and polished, but every-thing else she could see looked surprisingly the same — glazed institu-tional green block on the lower half of the wall, speckled beige paint on the block above. She shook off the reverie and kept walking, observing the flow of people, keeping an eye out for anything suspicious. "Where exactly are they setting up for the bake off? The cafeteria?"

"That'd be the obvious choice, wouldn't it? But no, the event will be in the gym. More room."

The gym was at the very end of the three-hundred-foot-long hallway. Walking into the large expanse, Morgan could almost hear the sound of basketballs bouncing, sneakers squeaking, and kids shouting. She smiled.

"That's good to see."

Morgan looked at Cal. "What?"

"The smile." He jostled her shoulder with his. "Tells me you're perking up after your disastrous start this morning."

Morgan rolled her eyes. "Whatever." She scanned the room. Six baking stations with counters, ovens, refrigerators, cook tops, mixers, and an assortment of utensils were spaced evenly across the gym floor, about ten feet apart. A large pantry had been formed out of several silver metal shelves off to the side. And what she guessed to be the judge's table was assembled about fifteen feet from the stations. The production crew was busy assembling lights and reflective shades near each of the baker's workspaces. All in all, quite an operation.

"Can I help you?" A tall, beefy, mid-twenty-something Goth-looking guy with a deep voice and heavy British accent approached. He was dressed head to toe in black, his shaggy shoulder length hair dyed blood red, and his tee shirt sported a Union Jack dancing under a full moon with a werewolf.

"You must be with Sassy McComas." Cal extended his hand in greeting. "I'm Caleb Joseph."

The man crossed his arms over his chest, arched an eyebrow, and looked them up and down. "Why? Because I'm British? Do you think we run in herds? Are all your friends lumberjacks?"

Cal and Morgan stared at him.

Goth Man suddenly burst out laughing and slapped a hand against his thigh. "Of course, I'm with Sassy! I'm yanking your chain, mate." He shook Cal's hand. "Damon Douglass. Queen Sass's assistant, confidante, and all around do-whatever-needs-to-be-done person. Good to meet you Caleb. I understand you're one of our local sponsors and helping with the organizational details."

"That I am. I'm also setting up the book signing for tomorrow. I thought we'd use the old library. Do you have any specific requests for Sassy?"

"Ah, yes, I remember. Mind if we talk about that in a bit?" He waved a hand around the room. "A little busy right now." He gave Morgan the once over. "And I see you brought the police with you? Is there a problem?"

"Captain Morgan Hart."

Damon looked at Cal. "Not very chatty this one, eh?"

"It's part of her charm."

"Is that what you Americans call it?"

Before Cal could reply, a loud crash rang out from the middle of the gym. A late-fortyish blonde woman wearing a bright blue apron over an equally bright orange dress, was standing with her hands on her hips, glaring down at the short, middle aged man in front of her. A ceramic bowl was in pieces on the floor between them, oozing chocolate. Damon rushed over and Cal and Morgan followed with Cal stage-whispering, "That's Sassy McComas."

Damon slipped an arm around the woman's shoulders. She shrugged it off and glared at him. He held his hands up and took a step back. "Only trying to help, love."

Sassy McComas continued to scowl at her assistant. "If you really want to help me, you'll do something about this hack."

"Now wait a minute," the man interjected. He flipped his shoulder length brown hair back and took a step toward Sassy. "Who are you calling a hack?"

"What *should* we call you?" Morgan asked stepping in between Sassy and the supposed hack.

"Benny Staples. And I'm not a hack." He squared his shoulders. "I trained at the Culinary Institute of America and graduated near the top of my class."

Sassy laughed, loud and forced.

Morgan noted the crew, while still busily working, were constantly sneaking peeks. She turned to Benny. "What's seems to be problem here?"

"*Queen* Sass here hurled that bowl at me."

"And why would she do that?"

Benny shrugged.

"Besides being a baker, Benny is also a food blogger," Damon offered up with a scowl. "Likely the reason is he's been busy lately writing nasty tripe about our sweet Sass, haven't you dear Benny?"

"What kinds of things?" Morgan asked glancing from Damon to Benny.

"All manner of terrible reviews about Queenie's Loquacious Cakes and Sassy herself." Damon crossed his arms. "He's been a real bugger about our queen."

"I can second that." Another baker walked up, a plump tidy-looking, thirty-something woman with a tight bun and an even tighter expression. "Benny's had it out for Queen Sass for a while now."

"And you are?" Morgan asked.

"Oh. Well." She waved a hand in the air. "I don't want to get involved. Call me an innocent bystander."

"You don't get to claim innocent bystander when you've inserted yourself into a conversation," Morgan said.

The aproned woman darted her eyes about and then leaned in and said in a low voice. "Meg. I'm Meg Chapel."

Benny held his hands up. "Look, I don't want any trouble. I'm only here to bake. Just because I happen to think Sassy here is a has-been, it has nothing to do with my participation." He squared his shoulders. "Besides, I'm allowed to have my own opinions. And write about them." He looked Damon and Sassy over. "Last I checked, we still have a First Amendment in *this* country." Benny shot Meg a nasty glance. "And how did you even get on this show? Your food might look good, but it tastes horrible." He looked at Morgan and explained, "She posts these delicious looking pics on Insta but everything she bakes tastes like cardboard."

"Well, that's just rude." Meg blinked hard and wiped at her eyes. "I'm an excellent baker. Sassy wouldn't have chosen me, otherwise."

"Oh, please." Benny rolled his eyes. "You got picked because they're looking for drama. Turns the ratings up." He motioned to another baker who'd been watching. "Paul come here. Tell them how bad Meg's baking is."

"I'm not getting involved," Paul called out from one of the kitchen stations, cracking walnut shells and picking out the nuts. "But yeah, I was on another show with Meg. She can't bake to save her life. But it can be entertaining to watch her try."

Meg shot Paul a glare. "I thought we were friends." She huffed and turned to Sassy. "Queen Sass, tell them it's not true." She looked pleadingly at the older woman. Sassy looked away.

"And it looks like the show is already getting plenty of drama." Morgan nodded toward a cameraman who had slipped in and was filming the exchange.

"Benny, why on earth would you want to be in a baking competition spearheaded by someone you obviously don't respect?" Cal asked.

Benny tilted his head. "I can think of ten-thousand reasons."

"He means the prize money," Cal said to Morgan.

She frowned at him. "Yeah, thanks, I got that." She turned to Benny and Meg. "Why don't you two go wherever you bakers go when you're not in here? Let things cool down a bit."

Morgan watched as Benny shot Sassy a not-so-nice look over his shoulder and noted she returned the favor. "So, Sassy? Are we good here?"

The older woman sniffed. "As good as can be expected when one is confronted by such a mannerless beast." Sass flipped her hair back and looked at Damon. "Be a love and get this cleaned up, would you? Before someone slips in this mess. Then get with the attorney and find me a loophole in the Baker's Dozen contract so we can purge ourselves of Mr. Benny Staples."

CHAPTER 3

Morgan sat down at her desk and stared for a moment at the computer monitor in front of her. It was well past lunch time when she dropped Cal off at the bookstore and was contemplating walking over to Dave's for a plate of French fries.

"How's the set up for the bake-off going?" JJ asked.

She swiveled her chair around. "Dramatic. We weren't there ten minutes when the host got into a fight with one of the contestants. Threw a bowl full of melted chocolate and everything."

"Hannah says bakers are a competitive breed, but could you imagine Hannah doing something like that?"

"Never in a million years."

"Though, to be honest, she does get pretty intense when we're playing Yahtzee." He grinned. "It's kind of adorable, though."

Morgan rolled her eyes. "Please. You're in love. *Everything* Hannah does is adorable."

"True enough." JJ laughed. "Anything we need to be worried about over there? Bijoux hasn't had the best summer."

"It's been a horrible summer. I was hoping the slide into fall would be quiet. Let's hope flying bowls will be the worst of it."

"Yeah. Hannah is pretty excited about participating. I hope nothing goes wrong for her sake."

"And it would be nice not to have any more dead bodies."

JJ scratched the back of his head. "True enough. Hannah wanted me to stop by the community center after work to show me the set up. She's so excited about everything. She's a huge fan of Queen Sass."

"Well, I'm happy for Hannah. But there's just something off about her royal highness."

"You got a vibe about Queen Sass?"

"Yeah, I got a vibe. Can you do a me a favor and run a search on her, see if anything turns up. A baker named Benny Staples, too. He was the recipient of the bowl full of chocolate." Her stomach growled. She checked her smart watch. 2 p.m. "In the meantime, I'm going to run over to Dave's. There's a grilled cheese and fries calling me."

ORIGINALLY BUILT during the tourist incursion of the 1950s, Dave's Diner was retro before retro was cool. Morgan slid into a red vinyl covered booth, rested her arms on the baby blue Formica tabletop, and stared out the window. Bijoux was busier than usual for this time of year. The summer season had ended a week ago, but the streets were crowded with people who were here for the bake-off. She and JJ would have be extra vigilant. *That means getting some sleep.* Her nightmares about Ian were getting more and more frequent and intense. Maybe she needed a vacation. Which was a little funny, considering she lived in a beach town.

"What you having, sunshine?"

Morgan looked up. Jerome the lanky, opinionated waiter stood at the ready to take her order. "Hey, Jerome. Grilled Cheese. Fries. Iced tea. Thanks." He shook his head before walking away. At least he was keeping his thoughts about her food choices to himself for the moment. *Now if only he could keep that judgmental look off his face.*

"What's on the daily special?" Cal asked as he slid into the booth seat opposite Morgan.

She glared at him. "Why are you here? I just dropped you off. Don't you have a shop to run? Art students to boss? Old ladies to charm?" The man was maddening in his ability to just show up, wherever she happened to be and insert himself into her day.

"My nephew, Henry, is here for the weekend," Cal said, perusing the menu. "He's in his last year of college, studying interior design, and crazy for this cupcake baking show. When he found out Bijoux was hosting it, he couldn't stay away." Cal smiled. "He's a good kid. Used to help out at the shop during summer vacations, so he knows the drill."

Jerome set a glass of iced tea in front of Cal and gave Morgan hers. "Usual?" Jerome asked.

"Nah, I think I'll shake it up. Reuben and fries today, please." Cal slid the menu back into its plastic holder.

Jerome raised an eyebrow. "No longer worried about your cholesterol levels, I see. Okay then," he said and left to place the order.

"First, how did I not know you had any siblings, let alone a nephew? Second, that doesn't tell me why you're here, sitting at my booth."

"Everything is an interrogation with you." He sipped his tea, made a face, and stirred in a packet of raw sugar. "Well, captain, I have one sister, Sara. She's eight years older, lives in Niles, and got divorced when Henry was about fifteen." He took another sip of tea. "Better. And, before you ask, no, she was not named for the Hall and Oates song."

"I wasn't going to ask."

"Well, for whatever reason, a lot of people do." He leaned forward and whispered. "It makes her a little crazy."

"I wouldn't know anything about that." Morgan rolled her eyes and smiled. She was often the recipient of silly jokes when people put *Captain* and *Morgan* together. "Crazy runs in the family, does it?"

"You have no idea." Cal leaned back and laughed. "I'm the sanest one and I ended up running a haunted bookstore in a small town where everyone knows everyone else's business."

"And don't forget your not-so-secret-secret-romance-novel writing career."

He snorted. "Plus, my soon to be launched police procedural writing career."

"You were serious about that?" She narrowed her eyes. "I'm telling you now, don't write about us."

"There's an 'us' now, is there?" He leaned in and wiggled his eyebrows up and down.

Morgan felt a blush creeping up. *Stop it. No blushing!* She feigned anger instead. "You know what I meant."

Jerome placed their orders in front of them, tsked at Morgan as she stuffed a fry in her mouth, and walked away.

Morgan was used to Jerome's attitude but it still it rankled her some. *So what if I like a good burger on occasion or fries or a slice of chocolate cake?* She took a bite of the sandwich and almost groaned in pleasure. "What's on the agenda for the bake-off?" she said around a mouthful of melted cheese and crispy fried bread.

"I have it in an email." Cal pulled out his phone and scrolled through the screen. "Let's see. A meet and greet around six today. Tomorrow, filming officially starts. Same with Saturday, though I'm hosting that book signing for Sassy in the afternoon. Sunday is the final day of shooting and the finale of the bake-off along with the crowning of the new Baker's Dozen Lord or Lady of Cupcakes."

"Lord or Lady? What's that about?"

"They play on the whole aristocratic/nobility shtick. At the end of each of the local weekend-long bake-off contests, someone is named Lord or Lady. This round happens to be the last before all the winners convene in New York. That's when they'll take part in the actual ten-episode series, competing against the other twelve weekend-bake-off lords and ladies. Whoever wins that is crowned Prince or Princess, gets a hundred-thousand dollars in prize money, plus thousands-of-dollars-worth of new baking appliances and gadgets. Rumor has it there might be a baking show for the winner this time around, too."

"Well, that certainly explains the tension and chatter around it. So, what's Sassy's angle?" Morgan asked dipping a fry in a glob of ketchup. "Besides the queen persona."

"I follow the show, but have no idea about her private life." Cal shrugged. "I just take the show, and her, for what they are. Entertainment."

"Please, you're one of the organizers of the event and a local sponsor. You have to know something."

A middle-aged bald man dressed in white burst into the diner. "Someone has got to help me! It's an emergency!"

Morgan jumped out of the booth and rushed up to the man. He was obviously in distress, breathing rapidly, his face bright red against his shirt.

Jerome ran out of the kitchen, his hand on his heart. "What?!? What happened?"

Morgan grabbed one arm and Jerome grabbed the agitated man's other arm. They helped him to a chair. Morgan squatted down in front of the red-faced man. "I'm the police captain. Can you tell me what's wrong?" she asked calmly, taking her phone out in case she had to call 911.

"Smoked paprika!"

"Smoked paprika?"

"Yes! I—I ran out of it. I'm in desperate need of it."

"Excuse me? Your emergency is smoked paprika?"

"Yes! It's an essential ingredient in my recipe and this godforsaken town has none!"

"Oh, for heaven's sake." Morgan tucked her phone into her back pocket and stood. "Who are you?"

"Pierre Brahman," Cal whispered in her ear.

Morgan jumped. "Dammit, Cal. What have I told you about sneaking up on me?"

He shrugged. "I'm getting stealthier, aren't I? Or are you getting lax? I would never have been able to sneak up on you when you first moved here."

He wasn't wrong. Beach living was making her soft. Lack of sleep, too. "What does that have to do with anything?" She shook her head. "Never mind."

"Pierre is Sassy McComas's sous chef and known for helping Sass develop the amazing flavors in her baked goods," Cal added.

She frowned at him.

"Just trying to help."

"Thanks for the information." She turned back to the red-faced chef. "Mr. Brahman, you can't barge in somewhere screaming you have an emergency when all you need is a spice."

Pierre straightened. "I must have it for my famous paprikash. I'm cooking it for Sassy's dinner, and she will not be denied the rich, smokey flavor she's come to love." He looked pleadingly at Jerome. "Sir, do you have any? Your grocery store is sorely lacking in all things paprika."

"Tom! Paprika emergency!" Jerome called out to Tom the cook.

"*Smoked* paprika," Pierre corrected.

21

Jerome gave Pierre an evil glare and stomped back to the kitchen to retrieve the spice. "I am not having this today," he muttered. "Not one bit."

"All right, problem solved Mr. Brahman," Morgan said. "In the future, I would ask that you not run through town screaming emergency, or I'll have to arrest you. Do you understand how dangerous that is?"

Pierre crossed his arms over his chest. "Not as dangerous as Sassy when she doesn't get her smoked paprikash."

"Nevertheless, you will conduct yourself with decorum while you are here in Bijoux. Do I make myself clear?"

Pierre nodded as Jerome handed him a small container.

"Is it smoked?"

"If it were anymore smoked, the state would be trying to put a tax on it," Jerome bit out.

"Good." Pierre stood, turned on his heel, and strode out of the diner.

"All right everyone, show's over," Morgan announced to the diner patrons who'd gathered to watch. "Please return to your meals." Which is what she wanted to do. Two public incidents and it was only the first day. She hoped this wasn't a preview of what was to come. *JJ and I will have to keep a close eye on things.*

CHAPTER 1

"IT'S BEEN A WEIRD DAY, Gris. I'll tell you that." Griselda sat opposite Morgan on her brown leather sofa, pawing at a loose thread on an orange throw pillow. She ruffled the cat's head, stood, and stretched. She'd stopped by her shotgun beachside cottage to change her clothes and feed the cat before heading over to the Bake-Off meet and greet. Her phone pinged. "Huh. It's Liz. She wants me to give her a call. Morgan looked at the cat. "Hopefully, it's some good news, eh Gris?"

The cat meowed and went back to licking her paw.

"My sentiments exactly." Morgan hit dial.

"Hey, girlfriend. How are you doing?" Liz asked.

"I'm okay. What's up?"

"I had an interesting conversation earlier today." Liz hesitated. "You might want to sit down."

Liz wasn't one for drama, so telling her to sit down had Morgan's stomach clenching. She started pacing instead. "Yeah, no. What's going on? You sound stressed."

"Because I am. I ran into an old informant of ours today. You remember Jacky? He was hanging around a street corner at 7 Mile and Gratiot. Said he was waiting for a bus, but you know that wasn't the case." Liz exhaled audibly. "Anyway, I'd asked him a while back to keep his ears open for any chatter about Ian."

Morgan rubbed her eyes. "Really? You think there could be chatter on the street, after all these years?" Even though Morgan was adamant she was going to solve Ian's murder, she'd run into dead ends everywhere and was more than frustrated by the lack of any breaks in the case. Jacky sounded like another dead end to add to the long list. "And why trust him?"

"Just my gut, Morgan. You know how that is."

"Yeah, yeah. I do. For sure. So, tell me. What did he say and why is he talking now?"

"Jacky's supplier was recently arrested. The supplier, in turn, revealed the head of their drug operation in exchange for witness protection. The head drug dealer was hauled in today. Jacky's worried that he, and the other lower level dealers, have a target on their backs now." She stopped, took a breath, and continued. "He's scared that he's going to get a bullet to the head and he wants protection in exchange for some info."

Morgan's stomach flipped and rolled. What—what did he say?" Morgan did sit now, her legs trembling so badly she worried she'd fall over. "Liz. Please tell me what you found out.

"Oh God, Morgan—He says it was James! Jacky told me it was James Wheat who killed Ian."

"No! Not possible." *Ian's partner? His friend? The guy who was supposed to have his back?* But somewhere, deep down, a voice whispered, *Yes, it's possible.*

"Jacky says James was in on their drug deals. Says he's dirty. He told me Ian found out and James killed him before Ian could report it."

"We need proof. More than just Jacky's word." Morgan rubbed the center of her chest to relieve the tightness. "Have you talked to Chief Smith? Smitty is pretty hardcore, old school. I don't know if she'd trust anything Jacky said."

"I mentioned to her it looked like I might have a break in the case but didn't drop too many details. Told her I'd vet my sources and let her know. I also wanted to talk to you before I got too deep into it with the chief." Liz paused and Morgan knew she was collecting her thoughts. "Did you ever find anything in Ian's things that seemed odd? Maybe there's something there you didn't catch the first time?"

"No, I don't think so. But it's also been a while since I went through everything...."

"I know this is hard for you, but maybe with what Jacky told me— well, it might give you a different perspective. It might help you discover something you may have overlooked before."

"Maybe. Maybe I *have* missed something." Morgan got up and strode down the hallway to the guest room where Ian's files and notes filled up fifteen bankers' boxes. After Ian had been killed, Liz had gone to his office for her to clear out his desk and personal items, even his *Star Trek* bobblehead collection. He also had kept case files at home, which Morgan had put in the boxes along with everything else when she moved, but she couldn't help but wonder if she'd bypassed something important.

Over five years and she'd gone through every last box, many times, hoping to find that one thing that would explain what happened the day he was murdered.

"I definitely will go through everything again," Morgan said. "Do you think they'll at least question James?"

"That could be a problem. He retired about six months ago. Smitty gave him a big send off. In her speech she wished him well in his retirement in the Caribbean. I didn't think anything of it at the time. It's not like he had kids or a wife to add to expenses over the years, so it seemed legit that he could save up and buy a condo on some resort island. Barbados, I think. But I did some digging and James has nothing on social media. Completely scrubbed. Nothing out there at all. You have to wonder why."

Morgan's stomach roiled. "James was Ian's mentor. He was our friend." Morgan fought back the tears. "He came over for dinner almost every Saturday night. We shared season tickets for the Red Wings for heaven's sake."

"I know, sweetie. I know."

"Liz, please keep it quiet on your end and don't talk to anyone just yet. Not even Smitty. I'll be in touch soon."

"Okay. Will do. And Morgan."

"Yes?"

"If you need someone, please reach out okay? I'm here. Frankie's there. And your dad too. Okay?"

"I'll be fine. Thanks Liz. I appreciate it." Morgan disconnected the call. She stumbled to the bathroom, soaked a washcloth in cold water, and held it over her face. *Breathe*, she told herself. *Slow, deep breaths.*

The front door opened, and Morgan jumped.

"Hey! I'm letting myself in." Francine 'Frankie' Whitaker, Morgan's childhood best friend and owner of the local dive, Perch Mouth Bar & Grille, called out.

"Just washing up. Give me a sec." Morgan hung up the wash cloth and turned, slapping a hand to her chest when she saw Frankie standing in the bathroom doorway.

"Dammit, Frankie! You scared the crap out of me! Creep around much?"

"I told you I was letting myself in." Frankie gave her a slight head-tilt and a sharp-eyed look. "You don't look so good."

"I'm tired of people telling me I look like crap," Morgan snapped, walking by her and striding to the kitchen.

"That's not what I said and you know it. I meant you look like you could use someone to talk to. Liz texted me—"

"Happy to hear you and Liz are staying in contact, even if it is to *talk about me behind my back.*" Morgan opened the fridge and pulled out a jug of iced tea and poured two glasses. She handed Frankie one and gulped down half of the other.

Frankie took a sip of hers and sat on one of the stools at the kitchen island. "I've known you since we were in kindergarten and I know when something has you unsettled, in spite of Liz's text. So spill it. I'm not budging until you do."

Fine. "Fine. Liz just called. She ran into an old informant of ours. The guy claims Ian was killed by his partner, James Wheat. Supposedly James was involved in drug dealings and Ian was going to turn him in. There. That's what's going on." She blinked back tears. "What the hell, Frankie?"

Frankie jumped off the stool and wrapped her arms around Morgan. "We'll get through this. If you didn't notice, I put a couple of bottles of wine in the fridge. I'll order up a pizza and we can talk. Do you want me to call Able?"

Morgan shook her head. "Thanks for the offer, but I can't stay here. I have to get over to the Bake-Off opening."

"I don't think so. I think you'll skip it, we'll stay in, drink wine, and I'll order us a pizza. What say you?"

"Honestly, I say that's the best thing I've heard all day." Morgan sighed, gave her friend a squeeze, then stepped back. "But I need to be at the community center tonight, keeping an eye on things."

"JJ's going to be there anyway because of Hannah. And I'm sure Cal will be on the look-out for trouble, given his knack for attracting it."

"I don't know, Frankie." Morgan ran through potential scenarios for mayhem: limp vegetables, cakes that didn't rise, angry competitors, and an irritated host. Those last two could turn into bigger issues.

Frankie crossed her arms and stared at Morgan. "When's the last time you had an evening to just 'be?'"

"It's been a minute."

"You need some time to process what Liz told you." Frankie said. "And you know I'm an excellent sounding board." She reached out and lay her hand on Morgan's shoulder.

Morgan allowed herself to relax a little. *Okay.* She really did need to unwind. She'd have to go through Ian's boxes as soon as possible again. But not tonight. She just couldn't bring herself to do it tonight. "You're right. JJ will be there. Cal will be there." What could possibly go wrong at a baking show? Just because the last two events that Cal organized ended up with multiple murders, doesn't mean this one will." At least she hoped not.

CHAPTER 5

"MORGAN? ARE YOU IN THERE?"

The pounding on her door and the man's voice cut through Morgan's sleep, ending another nightmare, the recurring one where she first saw Ian's dead body in the alley. She sat up. Shook off the dream, checked the clock. 6:30 a.m. *What the hell?* She pulled on sweats, rushed to the door, but Frankie beat her to it.

"I wasn't expecting to see you," Cal said.

"Yeah, good morning to you too," Frankie muttered. She looked at the two coffees in Cal's hands. "Since it's unlikely either of those are for me, I'm outta here." She pulled on her shoes and sweater and wrapped Morgan in a hug. "Call me." She kissed Morgan's cheek and grabbed her bag. "Later, Cal," she said and left through the front door.

Cal cleared his throat. "Frankie stay over last night?" He handed Morgan a coffee.

She snatched the waxed paper bag out of his hand, not waiting for him to hand it to her. "I hope there's something sugary in here." She walked around to the other side of the kitchen island and emptied the bag onto a paper plate. Ah. Dave's Deli chocolate glazed yeast donuts. *Perfect.* "Why are you here?"

Cal handed her a coffee and grabbed one of the donuts. "You weren't at the kick-off last night. I thought I'd stop by and make sure you were okay before the day got started. It's not like you to miss something like that." He took a drink of his coffee and sat on a stool opposite her. "But it looks like you had Frankie...?"

"Yes, I had Frankie." Morgan tilted her head. "What are you getting at?"

"Nothing, really." He took a bite of donut. "So, are you two dating now?"

"What?" Pounding at the front door interrupted Morgan's response. "Apparently Grand Central Station has been relocated to my house," she said striding to the door and opening it.

JJ was standing there, frozen in mid-knock. He dropped his hand. "We have a problem."

"What's going on?" Morgan motioned for her deputy to come in. She ran a hand through her hair, went back to the kitchen and her donut.

"Hey, Cal. You're here awfully early," JJ said, looking Cal up and down.

Cal pointed at Morgan's cup of coffee and donut. "Just bringing breakfast."

"Huh. Well, Cap'n you better take yours to go," JJ said, looking meaningfully at Morgan.

Morgan stared at JJ, her mouth agape. "You're kidding me," she said.

"I wish I was."

She sighed.

"Wait, what's going on?" Cal asked.

"Who is it?" Morgan said.

"Pierre Brahman, Sassy McComas's sous chef."

"Pierre Brahman?" Cal stood. "You mean Pierre is—"

"Dead," JJ finished.

"How? When?"

JJ shrugged. "Hannah called me. She found him in the alley behind the community center about twenty minutes ago. I jumped in the car, headed here to grab the captain on the way over."

He snatched the rest of Cal's donut off his plate and stuffed it in his mouth. JJ's phone pinged in his pocket. He checked his texts. "Doc McVie just got there. I called him right after I got off the phone with Hannah. Hannah's waiting just inside the back door until the captain and I get there. No idea beyond that."

Cal's phone pinged and he checked the message. "Looks like I won't be able to ride along. Henry locked himself out of the bookstore."

"Good," Morgan said, taking her donut with her to the bedroom to get dressed. "You weren't invited anyway."

"W̲ʜᴀᴛ ᴅᴏ ʏᴏᴜ sᴇᴇ, Dᴏᴄ?" Morgan asked as she and JJ strode into the alley behind the community center. The morning sun was still low in the sky and cast long shadows between the buildings. Sparse fog hugged the ground, leaving the air damp. Morgan was grateful it was early; it meant the usual curiosity seekers wouldn't be hounding them. And by people, she included her nemesis, Connie Graham.

Fleetwood McVie, named after his parent's favorite rock band, was Bijoux's family practice doctor/medical examiner/mortician and on-again-off-again boyfriend of said nemesis. "Well, nothing conclusive." He crossed his arms over his chest. "You know I don't like to guess, but I'm thinking poison. I'm getting a definite bitter almond scent from our victim." Doc crouched down and pulled the sheet away from the top half of the body.

"Poison? That's a new one." Morgan squatted down. Pierre was flat on his back, his left arm was twisted under his back and his right arm held tight to his chest, fingers clutching what looked like a half-eaten vanilla cupcake with bright pink icing and multi-colored sprinkles. Morgan snapped a few pics with her phone.

"Hannah, is this how he was when you found him?" When she didn't answer, Morgan looked up. Hannah was standing close to JJ and his arm was wrapped protectively around her shoulders. Her eyes were red and swollen, no doubt from crying. "I know this is hard and I'm sorry you were the one to find him." Morgan stood. "You were here early. What can you tell me?" She glanced at JJ. "Us. What can you tell us?"

Hannah took a steadying breath and let it out slowly. "Our call time is at 8:00 a.m., but I got here a little before 6 to see if the crew needed help with anything. I felt like I should help if I can, you know, since our town is hosting. Sassy came up to me and asked if I'd seen Pierre. I was making coffee for the crew and it was just about ready, so I think the time was about 6:15. She wanted to go over today's baking assignments. I told her I'd go look for him." Hannah's eyes filled with tears and she wiped at them.

"What made you think to look in the alley?" Morgan asked. "It's not a usual sort of place to go looking for someone."

JJ shot Morgan a slight frown. She ignored him.

"I checked the washrooms and the room off the little kitchenette that the crew uses as a breakroom. Then I remembered Pierre was a smoker so I went out front, then thought to check the alley and...." A fresh wave of tears spilled down Hannah's cheeks and JJ pulled her tighter into his side.

"Well, this is a cozy little gathering," Connie Graham said as she strolled up, Marie, her cameraperson behind her. Marie mouthed a silent *sorry* from behind Connie's back.

Morgan swung around to Doc, shooting him a narrow-eyed glare. "Did you tell Connie we had a body?"

Doc grimaced. "She may have overheard the call."

"I see you two are on again." Morgan shook her head. "Look, Doc, you have to stop with the pillow talk."

"Woodsy didn't do anything wrong," Connie interjected. "He's the best coroner in the county."

Morgan arched a brow. Doc was the *only* coroner in the county. Although he *was* good at his job, and thorough. Trouble was, he also had a big mouth.

"I didn't tell Connie anything." Doc shoved his wire rimmed glasses up the bridge of his nose. "She was snooping again."

"Woodsy!" Connie exclaimed. "Look Morgan, you can't blame me for wanting to make sure the citizens of Bijoux are fully informed when another maniac killer is on the loose."

"Nobody said anything about a maniac killer, Connie." Morgan blew out a breath. "Okay. Let's move this side-show along before the whole town shows up. JJ, will you please take Hannah inside?" JJ nodded and held the side door open for Hannah, then followed her in.

"Doc, process the body and let me know as soon as you know something."

"Captain Morgan, I didn't say anything to her," Doc added under his breath. "That's why we broke up three months ago. She was always undermining me."

"I heard that!" Connie huffed out.

"Connie, I have nothing for you right now," Morgan said. "We'll release an official statement when we have all the facts."

Connie flipped her bouncy blonde hair over her shoulder. "Oh, please, Morgan. Here you are, hiding information to your own benefit again."

"How is keeping *mis*information out of the news to my benefit?"

"So you can swoop in and be the hero at the end of the day." Connie sniffed. "Just like you did when we were kids. You have a savior complex. But you can't save everyone, can you, Captain?"

Morgan stared at Connie, reading her direct jab as a reference to Ian's killer never having been caught.

Doc gasped. "Connie you have stepped over the line. *Way* over."

"Well, I'm only trying to get to the truth," Connie said. "The Detroit Killer could be back in town as we speak. And the Romance Killer has recanted her confession. And who knows what will happen with the Psychic Killer. That person might very well escape before trial and murder us all in our beds!"

"Just go away, Connie. Go away before I arrest you for interfering with an ongoing investigation." Morgan walked up to the ambulance where Doc was packing up his equipment. "Where's Maggie? Do you need some help?" Maggie Cornet was Doc's young assistant who also carried an open crush on JJ.

"Maggie's visiting family in Traverse City. And yes, some assistance would be nice." He inclined his head to the sheet-draped body. "As you can see, Mr. Brahman was not a small man."

"I'll get JJ." Morgan turned and walked into the community center. *Damn! Damn! Damn!* Another murder. And this time she was going to have to question her deputy's girlfriend.

"JJ, would you please go help Doc? Maggie's out of town and he could use some help bagging the body and getting it into the ambulance."

JJ nodded. "Sure." He gave Hannah's arm a squeeze. "I'll be right back."

Morgan sat in the chair JJ had vacated and turned it to face Hannah. They were off in a quiet corner of the gym for privacy, far away from the activity of the crew as they finalized everything for the start of the bake-off. "I really am sorry you had to see that. It's not an easy thing."

"I don't know how you and JJ do this on a regular basis." Hannah pulled a tissue out of her pocket and wiped at her nose. "Is there anything I can do to help? I mean, I've told you everything, but if there's anything else…?"

Morgan pulled out her phone and showed Hannah the picture of the cupcake. "Can you confirm if this is one of your wrappers on the cupcake?"

Hannah looked at the image and turned white.

"Pierre and Doc are on their way to the morgue," JJ said walking back in. "What happened?" he asked, squatting beside Hannah's chair.

Hannah continued to stare at the photo. JJ followed her gaze, then his eyes locked with Morgan's. "What's that about?"

"It's the cupcake Pierre was holding when he died. I'm asking Hannah to confirm whether or not this is her signature wrapper."

"We are not doing this."

Morgan's eyes narrowed. "Yes, we are, JJ. Hannah, please answer the question."

"Don't say anything," JJ said. "I'll call a lawyer for you."

Hannah seemed to shake off her initial shock. And shook her head. "Why? I didn't do anything wrong." She looked at Morgan and nodded. "Yes, that's one of my wrappers. I didn't even notice it when I found—him. Turquoise and, if you look closely, you'll see the shop name in the folds."

"Do you have any idea how Pierre got one of your cupcakes?"

"I brought in a couple dozen for the crew. Put them in the cafeteria when I got here." Hannah clapped a hand over her mouth. "Oh my god. You think someone poisoned him with one of my cupcakes?"

JJ threw up his hands. "Why are you doing this to her?" he asked Morgan.

"I'm not doing anything *to her*. Do I need to remind you we have a case to solve? JJ, I'd like you to go retrieve those cupcakes from the cafeteria. And find out if anyone else ate any of them and aren't feeling well."

He ignored Morgan. "C'mon, Hannah. I'm taking you home."

"*Deputy*, do I need to put you on leave and call in my uncle to assist with this investigation?" Morgan's, Uncle Arnie Hart, was her dad's twin brother and the Odawa County Sheriff.

"You are not taking me home." Hannah dug in, her expression firm. "The competition starts soon. I'm baking today." She poked him in the shoulder. "And you're going to get yourself together. If you're so worried about things, then get to work and prove I'm innocent."

"But you've just been through a horrible experience." JJ ran a hand through his hair.

"Yes, I have. And I'm going to deal with it in the best way I know how. Create something beautiful and delicious."

"What's going on?" Sassy asked as she walked up to Morgan. She looked at Hannah. "Did you find Pierre?"

Hannah started tearing up again.

Morgan stepped forward. "Sassy, I'm sorry to have to tell you this, but Pierre is dead. Hannah found him in the alley about an hour ago."

Sassy's hand flew to her chest and she stumbled. JJ grabbed a chair and helped her sit.

"Is there anyone we can call for you?" Morgan asked.

Sassy nodded. She looked at JJ. "Please. Be a dear and get Damon for me? I think he's in the library." She turned to Morgan. "How?"

"We don't know for certain yet. The M.E. will do his exam today."

"He was poisoned!" Hannah blurted out. Morgan shot her a look and she fell silent.

"Like I said, we don't know the cause of death for certain," Morgan repeated.

Sassy frowned. "If it truly was poison, you can bet Benny Staples did it."

"Why would you say that?"

"He wanted Pierre's job. The weasel had been trying to talk me into giving him a go at it."

"You didn't mention that when you were fighting with him."

"Well, why would I?" Sassy fanned her face with her hand. "I do not want to talk about this."

Damon returned with JJ, squatted down next to Sassy, and handed her a cup of tea. "I heard what you said, Sassy." He looked up at Morgan. "Benny and Sass have a bit of a paramour history and it's painful for her to talk about it. So, we don't." Damon patted Sassy's hand. "JJ told me about Pierre. What a terrible tragedy for the show."

"A tragedy for the show? How about his family?" Morgan asked.

Sassy sniffed and Damon handed her a tissue. "*We* were his family," Sassy said. "Now if you don't mind, I need to let the bakers and crew know Pierre is gone."

CHAPTER C

MORGAN GLANCED at JJ out of the corner of her eye while she drove through town. He hadn't said a word since they left the crime scene, just stared straight ahead, didn't even wave at people on the street as he usually did. "Look," she began.

JJ held up a hand. "I already know what you're going to say."

"Really? And what do you think that'd be?"

He sighed. "We have a job to do, and we can't let our personal emotions interfere."

Morgan nodded. "That's part of it. The other part is I want you to know I realize this is hard for you." She patted his arm. "But Hannah isn't a suspect at this point, so you can relax."

She felt him do the exact opposite and stiffen. She dropped her hand.

JJ turned slightly in his seat. "What do you mean, 'at this point?' You know she had nothing to do with Pierre's death."

Morgan pulled the truck up in front of the station, parked, and shut off the engine. She faced JJ. "What do I always say?"

His mouth was in a tight line. "Everyone is a suspect until they're not."

"Absolutely. I will take you off this case if I have to, JJ. Believe that," Morgan said. She exited the truck and walked around to the passenger side, where JJ still sat, and leaned on the door. "Go run some searches on Pierre Brahman. See if you can find any connection to Benny Staples beyond hearsay. Check with Doc and ask if anyone else had an issue after eating one of Hannah's cupcakes. Or if the remaining ones checked positive for poison."

"You mean dead. Not an 'issue.' Dead. As in if anyone else died from Hannah's food."

Morgan rolled her eyes. "Don't be so dramatic. I think if anyone else died, we would have already heard about it. This feels more targeted. Having said that, I could imagine someone putting just enough poison in the others to make anyone else who ate one sick. Maybe trying to throw us off."

Morgan pushed away from the truck and noticed the long line-up outside Hal's Hardware Store, Bijoux's Unofficial Center of the Universe. The line-up wasn't due to a new electric drill or a big sale on lumber. Nope. It was coffee cake. Zoe's coffee cake to be precise. Morgan's stepmom baked a huge coffee cake every Wednesday and served it up free with a cup of freshly brewed coffee to anyone who came into the store. "I'm betting Mayor Ed is at Dad's. I'm going to head over, let him know we have a potential murder. Please get to work. Maybe it'll help to keep your mind occupied. I'll check in with you later."

"Captain?"

"Yeah?"

"I wouldn't mind some cake, if there's any left." He stretched. "Maybe two pieces. It's been a rough morning. I'd like to be prepared with an extra slice in case I need it later."

Morgan smiled. That's the JJ she knew. "I'll see what I can do."

She crossed the street and stopped outside the door to Hal's, noticed there were more people in line than usual. Zoe must have a new recipe. "Excuse me," Morgan said to a man blocking the entry. "Would you please let me by?"

"No cutters." He spun around and faced Morgan. Well, teetered might be a better description.

"Mr. Dominic?" No wonder she didn't recognize him from behind; the septuagenarian had dyed his stark white hair an unnatural shade of red. "I didn't realize that was you."

He patted his head. "Because I look thirty years younger, right? That's what my new GF tells me." Using his cane for balance, he leaned in closer to Morgan and stage-whispered, "GF means girlfriend."

"Oh-kay then. Would you mind letting me pass?"

"Nope. No cutters. You know the rules."

"Honestly, Mr. Dominic, how many times have we been through this? That's my dad in there. I'm not cutting." She gestured toward the door. "I'm visiting."

Mr. Dominic sighed and waved his cane. He wobbled and the person in line behind steadied him. "Fine, go, eat your cake ahead of all of us starving people." People around him started grumbling.

Ignoring the chants of *"cutter"* behind her, Morgan entered the hardware store. The aromas of wood, metal, and paint blended together into the familiar tangy scent she'd known since childhood. She walked down the power tool aisle, the wood floor creaking beneath her boots and headed toward the back of the store where her dad and Zoe had set up a makeshift coffee bar and serving area. Mayor Ed was standing off to the side, engaged in what looked like a heated debate with an attractive older woman she didn't recognize, though she did look a bit like Ed around the eyes—average height and toned like a yoga instructor, with caramel-colored hair in a loose chignon that complemented her light brown eyes, dressed in brown tights, a longish green tunic, and an intricately knit purple wool shawl.

"Excuse me. May I have a word, Mayor?" Morgan asked, interrupting the argument.

Ed glared at her for a moment, then his expression relaxed. "Of course." He nodded toward the woman he was arguing with. "Morgan, this is my younger sister, Wendy Peltier. She's just moved to Bijoux and is opening a yarn shop in that vacant space on the other side of Hannah's. Wendy, this is Morgan Hart, our police captain."

"And my amazing daughter," Able called from the other side of the coffee bar where he and Zoe were handing out hot beverages and what appeared to be a chocolate coffee cake. Morgan would definitely have to make sure she got a few slices when she was done with Ed.

"And my fabulous stepdaughter," Zoe said.

Morgan smiled. "It's nice to meet you. I'm certain your yarn shop will be a great addition to Main Street," Morgan said, extending her hand. "I used to crochet. Grandma Olga, my mom's mom, taught me when I was little. I used to make outfits for the family cat. I could use a distraction in the evenings. Maybe I'll take it up again."

"I'm sure your cat loved that." Wendy laughed and shook

Morgan's hand. "You'll definitely have to stop in and visit." She gave her brother a nasty look. "Assuming I can ever get opened. Ed here is insisting I fix up the exterior beforehand. I happen to like it just as it is."

"*That* is an ongoing disagreement in Bijoux between our fine mayor here and a good portion of the shop owners. Maintain that stance and you'll be considered a member of the Hold-Outs."

"We'll finish this discussion later," Mayor Ed said to Wendy. He stepped a few feet away and motioned for Morgan to follow.

She excused herself and took a deep breath. "We had a body turn up in the back alley at the community center earlier this morning. Pierre Brahman, part of the baking team," she whispered. "Doc is doing his exam, but the initial thought is the victim was poisoned."

His face turned bright red. "You can't be serious," he sputtered.

"I wish I weren't. JJ and I have started our investigation. I'll keep you updated."

"Yes, you will. And Captain? Solve it fast. We have a national spotlight on us right now with this baking show in town. I don't want Bijoux to suffer because of it."

"And you want justice for the deceased."

Ed threw his hands up in the air. "Sure. Whatever. Just handle it."

Morgan exited Hal's with several plastic wrapped pieces of coffee cake in hand and a chorus of boos and jeers from the line.

"Really, Morgan?" Beau Cornet, Morgan's former high school boyfriend turned town butcher, said as she passed him. "You disappoint me."

"Then it's good disappointing you isn't one of the things I worry about in life." She left him sputtering as she crossed the street, entered the police station, and handed JJ two pieces of coffee cake. "As ordered," she said with a smile.

"Did you get one of those for me?" Cal asked as he walked in.

Morgan rested a hand on her hip. "And why would I do that?"

"Come on. You knew I'd show up eventually. There's a potential murder investigation going on." He rested his elbows on the front counter. "Notice I said *potential*. Give me the deets."

"You did not just say 'deets.'"

"I believe I did. It means details."

"I know what it means. What begs to be understood is why you're talking like that." Morgan considered him. There was something going on here and she couldn't quite put her finger on it.

"He's in character," JJ said from his desk as if he had read her mind. "He's pretending to be his lead detective from his new book." He scooped up a bite of cake and stuffed it in his mouth. "What's his name? Flippy McDoo?"

Morgan burst out laughing and had to sit down. Caleb straightened, pushed up his black horn rimmed glasses, and crossed his arms. One of his tells, Morgan knew, when he was irritated. "Oh, relax, Professor," she said between giggles.

"The main protagonist's name is Philip McDonald and he's a highly decorated homicide detective." He shook his head and frowned. "Flippy McDoo? Really?"

JJ's computer pinged, announcing an incoming email. "Doc just sent over his notes." He opened the file, scanned through the PDF. "Murder it is, Captain. As suspected, cyanide poisoning." He glanced over at Morgan, frowning. "And yes, the cupcake was laced with it."

"Did any of the others test positive for cyanide?"

JJ read for a moment, then shook his head. "None. It was just the one Pierre had."

"Okay, so it *was* targeted. Have you turned up any of the other information we discussed?" Morgan asked.

"Not really. I'm still running searches."

"I did a little digging myself," Cal said. Both Morgan and JJ looked at him. "What? I have internet." He pulled his phone out of his pocket and opened the browser. "Benny isn't just gunning for Queen Sass, he was blasting Pierre Brahman too. Several of his blogs over the past six months claimed Pierre was doing a lousy job scrutinizing the Bake-off competitors' recipes and failing to weed out the fraudsters who were supposedly nicking ideas and techniques from other bakers." He held up his phone. "It's all here, but not on his usual blog. He posted this one on a private baking page I just happen to belong to."

"Private baking page?" Morgan asked. "You're not a baker. You're barely even an eater."

"I happen to like reading recipes. It helps relax my brain when I'm stuck on a scene."

"I had no idea you suffered from writer's block," Morgan said.

"Maybe Cal has trouble with the sex scenes," JJ suggested. "Isn't sex the biggest issue?"

"I do NOT have issues with sex—I mean *writing* sex scenes," Cal huffed out, slipping his phone into his tweed jacket pocket. "And how do you know anything about writing let alone romance writing?"

"I had to peruse all the course materials for that romance writers' conference back in May," JJ countered. "You know, on account of the two back-to-back murders? One of the workshops was all about writing steamy sex scenes and how to break the barrier of 'the dreaded block.'"

Morgan bit her lip to keep from laughing out loud at Cal's indignant glare. "You can't blame JJ for being thorough in our investigations," Morgan added in a dead-pan tone.

"Look, we're getting way off topic here. I just handed you a motive for murder on Benny's part," Cal muttered. "So instead if disparaging my profession, how about getting back to the investigation at hand?"

Morgan pushed up from her chair. "Agreed. And with that in mind, I'm going to head over to the bake-off, and talk to Benny and the other bakers. Keep me posted, JJ."

"You got it, Cap'n."

Cal drummed his fingers on the counter. "I'm coming with you."

"No you're not. This is police business," Morgan shot back.

"I just uncovered something that could blow your investigation wide open. Besides I'm working on a detective series, remember? I need to get up close and personal."

"He makes a good point, Cap'n," JJ interjected. "I mean, Cal might have some insight when you're questioning Benny."

Morgan rubbed a hand over her eyes in frustration. "Fine. You can come with me. But stay invisible." No sooner were the words out of her mouth that Morgan realized the futility of what she'd just said. If there was one thing she knew for certain about Caleb Joseph, it was that he was determined to stick his nose into police business every chance he got.

CHAPTER 7

THE BAKE-OFF WAS CLOSED to spectators, so the community center gym bleachers were mostly empty except for a couple of crew members taking a breather. The six bakers were all hard at work at their individual stations icing and decorating, and didn't look up when Morgan and Cal walked in. Damon approached. Still dressed in skinny black jeans but today he was wearing a Cult t-shirt under a black polka-dotted shirt. "Captain. Caleb. How can I help you?" he whispered.

"I'd like to talk with you about Pierre," Morgan replied.

"It'll have to wait. We're in the home stretch of today's Super Bake. Each baker has to create and decorate three dozen cupcakes in three different designs and flavors in just three hours." He checked the time on his phone. "There's less than an hour left before they have to present their work to the judges. One baker will then be eliminated today." He looked out over the gym. "If you haven't noticed, it's a little tense in here. It's one of my jobs to help keep the bakers calm."

Morgan crossed her arms. "As long as you cooperate, we shouldn't need much time at all."

Damon sighed dramatically. "What could you possibly want to know? I have no idea 'who dunnit.'" He said the last two words with air quotes.

"For starters, is there anyone else who had an issue with Pierre? Besides Benny? Can you think of any reason why someone might want him out of the way?"

"Nothing that I haven't already told you. Sassy thinks Benny did it. I'd leave it at that."

"I did a little digging," Cal said. "Besides criticizing Pierre on various baking forums, Benny has been brandishing hateful rhetoric against Queen Sass in his own food blog lately."

"Brandishing?" Morgan asked. She shook her head and refocused on Damon. "You haven't actually told me much of anything," she countered. "And taking someone's word for 'who dunnit,' rather than actual evidence, isn't how I work."

"What do you know about Benny's blog?" Cal asked. "I find it difficult to imagine you aren't aware of it."

"Of course, I'm aware of it. It's *my job* to be aware of anything that concerns Queen Sass," Damon hissed.

"What's going on? We're in the midst of a show here," Sassy said in a low voice as she walked up. An older, regal looking woman in a teal dress and perfectly coifed silver gray bouffant followed close on her heels.

"I'm investigating the death of your sous chef." Morgan considered her. "Which you don't seem upset about."

"Of course, I'm upset. I'm devastated by the loss of Pierre. What a horrible thing to say to me." She sniffed and Damon handed her a tissue from his studded black leather shoulder bag. "But I have a show to run." She dabbed at her nose. "Pierre would have wanted me to carry on."

"It's true. Pierre was loyal to no one but Queen Sass," the other woman said in a thick Scottish brogue.

"And you are?" Morgan asked.

"That's Bean Pierce, the Duchess of Spice," Cal said out of the corner of his mouth. "She's one of the judges and well known for her—as you've probably already guessed—spice combinations."

"Why don't you let people answer for themselves?" Morgan said. She turned to Bean. "You knew Pierre?"

"She tried to steal him away from me, on more than one occasion," Sassy said. She considered the other woman. "Come to think of it, didn't you threaten him once or twice yourself?"

Bean waved a hand. "Ah, don't be ridiculous. Just silly words between friends." One of the bakers raised a hand. "I'll see to their need," she said. "Carry on without me."

Another baker requested assistance and Sassy and Damon both turned and left Morgan and Cal without a word.

"Well, that was odd," Morgan said. "Let's go have a look around. I'll question the bakers as soon as they're done with this round."

THE FORMER GRADE school cafeteria was connected to the gym with a set of swinging double doors, no doubt originally set up so the students could run and play as soon as they were done eating. Tables were arranged into a large circle and chairs were neatly tucked beneath them. Behind the food line were Elise and Steven Bellamy, Hannah's parents, and owners of the Firefly, one of Bijoux's most popular bed and breakfasts, equally well known for its iconic pink façade.

Elise and Steven were both wearing white chef jackets and preparing food. "I wonder what they're doing here. And what could they possibly be cooking?" Morgan said to Cal.

"Probably lunch for the crew. The bakers will likely come in here to wait once they finish presenting their cupcakes for this round and wait while the judges deliberate," Cal replied.

Morgan nodded. "Hi Elise. Steven," she said.

They glanced up and smiled as they kept chopping vegetables, not missing a beat. Morgan would have lost a couple of fingers by now.

"Oh, Morgan, we're so glad you're here. You'll make sure nothing else bad happens, right?" Elise said. She suddenly stopped chopping and her tone shifted. She stared hard at Morgan. "And you'll make sure our Hannah is cleared of any wrongdoing, won't you?"

Steven stopped chopping as well and also stared at Morgan, holding his knife straight up in his hand.

"Look," Morgan began, but Cal cut her off.

"The captain knows how hard this is for both of you. Hannah too. It's good you're here so you can provide support as she competes."

"Why exactly are you here?" Morgan asked the couple.

"We were hired to do the food service. Productions like this will usually pick up local chefs and cooks, rather than travel with a large crew," Steven said.

"So, you're setting the menu?"

"Well, Pierre was doing that. We have his rough outline; he didn't get a chance to finish it," Elise said, frowning.

"May I see it?"

"Sure." Elise picked up a piece of paper from the back counter and slid it under the sneeze guard to Morgan.

Morgan studied the print-out. Nothing out of the ordinary, except for a scribbled note at the bottom left corner. The handwriting was difficult to read, but it appeared to say 'meet,' '5:30 a.m.,' and another word in between Morgan couldn't make out.

"Bean. It says Bean," Cal said from over her shoulder. "Meet Bean 5:30 a.m. Poor sentence structure."

Morgan turned, arching a brow at Cal. "But a possible clue to his murder. Hannah found him a little after 6:15, that would have been almost an hour after meeting with Bean."

"I see your cop brain ticking. What are you thinking?"

"I'm thinking you have a pesky habit of creeping up on me and reading over my shoulder."

"Really? I'm in your thoughts that much, am I?" He grinned. "But getting back to the matter at hand—are you thinking Bean Pierce had something to do with Pierre's murder? She's old enough to be my grandmother."

"Poison is an easy weapon to wield."

Cal turned serious. "And, based on my research, the murder weapon of choice for women killers."

"Exactly." Morgan set her mouth in a firm line. She texted JJ, asking him to run a search on Bean. "Come on. I need to have a private conversation with the Duchess of Spice."

CHAPTER 8

MORGAN AND CAL quietly slipped back into the gym to observe the proceedings. Each baker was standing at their station, while the camera crew filmed a slow pan of a long table laden with elaborate displays of cupcakes. Morgan's stomach growled and she clamped a hand over it.

"Skip lunch again?" Cal whispered.

"Actually, no. Wait. Maybe." She shook her head. "I've lost track."

Cal's eyes met hers and she saw that small spark of worry she'd noted yesterday reigniting.

"I'm fine. Stop looking at me like that. I get involved with a case and forget to eat. You've met me. This is not a new thing." She nodded toward the baking set-up. "So, what are they doing?"

"It's judgment time. Each baker will be questioned by the judges on their creations and the inspiration behind them."

"You really do have a lot of information packed into that head," Morgan observed.

"This show has been around for about ten years and the format hasn't changed much. Henry and I used to watch it together when he visited."

Morgan smiled. "You're really close to your nephew, aren't you?"

"Not as much as we once were, growing up plus his move to Indiana for college, does that." He sighed. "Life has an annoying habit of forging ahead when we're not looking or paying attention."

She considered Cal. He carried a certain wisdom beneath his staid-quirkiness. And she couldn't disagree; maybe it was time to move on with her own life. Maybe if she did, the nightmares would stop, and she could find some peace. After all, Ian's messages in her dreams had consistently been 'let it go.' *I can't do that until James Wheat is behind bars.* Her stomach churned, but this time not because she'd skipped lunch. She needed to sort through all of Ian's belongings one more time. She had to find something that could give them the proof they needed to put Wheat away.

"Benny Staples, would you please step forward?" Sassy asked. Two camera people followed the movement of Benny Staples, from two different angles, as he approached the dais. Sassy pointed to a plate with three single cupcakes on it. "Please, tell us your flavors and your inspiration."

Benny cleared his throat. "Since we were given free rein to choose the theme for this round of bakes, I chose the winter holidays. It's my favorite baking time of the year." He pointed at the tray. " Cupcake number one is a dark chocolate cupcake with a filling of roasted chestnut-and-salted-caramel puree and topped with a salted-caramel buttercream frosting, sprinkled with dark chocolate shavings. Number two is a candy-cane confection with a triple-vanilla bean cupcake topped with a white frosting and sprinkled with bits of crushed candy canes. And my pièce de resistance is inspired by everyone's least favorite holiday treat—fruit cake. But I can assure you, this cupcake will not be sitting in anyone's pantry for long. It's packed with a unique dried fruit-and-nut chocolate bark—dried cranberries and cherries that were pre-soaked in my special brandy reduction, tossed with walnut halves and added to a melted swirl of fine dark chocolate, then frozen to form a bark. The finished bark was then roughly chopped and blended into a brandy-and-golden-brown-sugar-cupcake batter. The finale is a creamy custard frosting drizzled with a brandy glaze and topped with a cherry."

Sassy sliced each cupcake in half, plated both halves, and handed one of the plates to Bean. They both took a fork and began to pick apart the cupcakes as though they were dissecting frogs in tenth-grade biology class. Various grunts, hmms, and huhs, emanated from the women as they tasted the cupcakes, rolling the bites in their mouths.

"Benny, did you happen to taste your fruitcake cupcake?" Bean asked.

"What do you mean?"

"You didn't answer the question, so we'll assume the answer is no."

Sassy shook her head. "It's quite claggy, underbaked." She wiped her hands on a napkin. "The other two are barely acceptable."

"Not exactly a grand celebration of the holidays, is it? Bean added.

"I'd say it's more of a dreaded visit from the ghost of Christmases past," Sassy quipped. "Thank you, Benny. You may return to your station."

Red-faced and scowling, Benny spun on the ball of his foot and stomped back to his work area.

"That didn't go well," Morgan said to Cal. The assistant director shushed her, and Morgan lowered her voice to a whisper. "Are they always this cutting?"

"Absolutely. Rumor has it Queen Sass is on the hunt for a break-out baking star for a new show she's developing. So far she hasn't found any likely candidates at the previous weekend bake-offs. But whoever makes an impression on her this weekend, whether they win or not, might have a shot at the spot."

"And you're just now telling me this? It could point to motive." Morgan rubbed her forehead. "Maybe. Somehow."

"It didn't seem relevant." He waved a hand. "I know you have to consider every angle, but I think you might be stretching it here."

"Stretching it how? What if we have a killer seeking to eliminate possible competition for the new show?"

"But it wasn't a competitor who was killed, it was Pierre, who already worked for Queen Sass."

"That's my point exactly. Pierre might have stood between the killer and success, hence the motive for murder." She angled her head to regard him. "You know if you want to make your police procedural authentic, you need to start thinking like a real cop."

Cal opened his mouth to reply but was cut off by another loud shush from the assistant director.

"Meg, you're up next. Please step forward," Bean called out this time.

Meg Chapel, the baker accused of being unable to bake, made her way to the judge's table. She ran her hands down her apron and took a deep breath. "Since it's September, I chose fall as my theme. The first is a cranberry vanilla cupcake with orange swiss meringue icing. Two is a double-fudge chocolate with white chocolate ganache filling and cacao nibs. Three is a gingerbread with pear filling and cream cheese frosting. They all remind me of baking with my grandmother," she finished, out of breath.

"Well, Meg, it seems you've been practicing," Sassy observed as she sniffed the cranberry cupcake and took a bite. "Well done."

"I concur," Bean added. "These are all delicious. Good job, Meg."

Meg beamed as she walked back to her station. The scowl on Benny's face, directed at Meg, wasn't lost on Morgan. The man definitely had some anger issues. *I wonder if they run deep enough to kill.*

Three more of the remaining bakers had presented their wares and now it was Hannah's turn.

"Tell us what you have for us today, Hannah," Sassy said.

Hannah smiled. "I've recreated three of my bakery's bestsellers. Triple Mochaccino, a dark chocolate cake, whipped milk chocolate frosting, coffee crème center, and vanilla sprinkles. The other is what I call my Mexican Wedding Cake, a spicy cinnamon and chocolate sponge, dark chocolate Swiss meringue topping with chopped candied ginger. The third is Pure Vanilla and, as the name suggests, vanilla flavoring through and through, including a wash of vanilla vodka."

"These are all lovely," Bean said. "I especially enjoy the hint of vodka."

Sassy laughed at the duchess. "As you would. Well done, Hannah."

When the tasting was done, Damon wrangled the bakers into the cafeteria. They sat at the circle of tables and Elise and Steven brought out a tray of half-sandwiches and veggie sticks along with three kinds of dips in individual ramekins, and small brown-paper bags of hand-cut kettle chips, lemonade, and bottles of water. The bakers passed along a stack of plates and napkins and helped themselves to the food and beverages. The tone was somber.

Morgan's stomach growled again. There was enough food to feed a small army. She straddled a chair. "Are all of you always this quiet after judging?" she asked.

Paul looked up. "We're reliving those last moments, going over in our heads how we could have done better. It's grueling out there."

"I'm sure it is. I have a few questions, then I'll leave you to unwind." She looked around the table. "Did any of you see Pierre yesterday morning?"

"You mean…before he—?" Meg asked.

"Yes. Before." Morgan noticed Hannah was avoiding eye contact, focused on her sandwich. Her mom, however, was hovering nearby and staring Morgan down. *Okay, then.*

"It wasn't necessary for any of us to be here before 8," Benny said. "Hannah is the only one who showed up so early."

That made Hannah look up. "Hey, I was only trying to help out."

"Help Pierre straight out the door from the looks of it." Benny snorted. "What's your angle? You looking for a sous chef job with Sassy?" His eyes narrowed. "Possibly trying to get on the queen's new show?"

Hannah's face turned red, but Morgan noted it was from anger, not embarrassment. "Absolutely not. What are you insinuating?"

"Let's drop this back a few notches, okay?" Morgan interrupted the argument. "Do any of you recall Pierre fighting with anyone?" The six bakers all shook their heads. This was going nowhere, fast.

"It's time, bakers," Damon called out from the doorway. The bakers all looked warily at each other before following the assistant back into the gym, Morgan and Cal close behind.

"Good luck," Morgan whispered to Hannah. "I know you're going to do great. JJ sends his luck and love, too."

Hannah smiled gratefully and mouthed *thank you.*

"Please form a line here, in front of the judging table," Damon directed, pointing at small pieces of barely discernible masking tape on the wood floor.

When everyone was on their mark, Sassy and Bean entered the room, beaming. "I'm so very proud of each and every one of you," Sassy began. "You've all done a wonderful job. Most of you, that is. Now, one of you will be named the winning baker in today's bake-off and one of you will be packing up and going home."

"I have the honor of announcing our first winner," Bean said. "This baker created some breathtaking combinations with chocolate, coffee, and chili peppers." She smiled and paused, dragging the moment out for the cameras. "Today's winning baker is…Paul."

The bakers applauded and Paul beamed. "Thank you so much," he said, placing a hand over his heart. "I'm shocked, really."

"Nonsense, your confections were delectable," Sassy said.

"Cheers to you, Paul," Damon added.

"Which means I have the unfortunate job of announcing the baker who will be leaving the competition," Sassy said. "And that baker is …" She paused and took a deep breath. "Benny."

"What?" Benny shouted. The cameras trained on his face. "What do you mean I'm leaving?"

Damon approached and put a hand on the man's shoulder. "Come along, Ben. Today is not your day."

Benny locked eyes with Sassy. "This is your doing. Getting even with me, aren't you?"

"I am doing no such thing." Sassy planted her hands on her hips.

"It was ultimately my decision," Bean interjected. "Your cupcakes had soggy bottoms and were underbaked. Such a mish-mash of trying too hard and failing miserably." She straightened and stared down her nose at the baker. "Now suck it up and move along. Have some pride, man. You're making a terrible spectacle of yourself."

Benny allowed Damon to turn him toward the exit. "You're both has-beens. Unworthy of judging my work," he shot over his shoulder. "I'm happy to be rid of you and this tired show."

"Cut!" the director yelled. "Everyone, take a break while we set up for the next bake."

Morgan whistled through her teeth. "That was something."

Cal shook his head. "Everyone knows Benny is a hothead, but this display was outrageous, even for him."

Morgan called out to Bean. "Bean, may I have a word with you?"

Bean turned and smiled, though Morgan noted it didn't quite reach her eyes. "Of course, Captain," she said as she approached. "How may I help you?"

"Pierre had made a note on yesterday's menu to meet you at 5:30 a.m. Can you tell me about that?"

"Only that it never happened."

"Excuse me?"

"He was supposed to meet me in the cafeteria. He wanted to chat over a cup of coffee. He never showed up."

"Was that a usual thing for him? It seems like you knew him fairly well," Cal said.

She waved a hand. "Oh, barely, really. So I can't say. Though I did find it odd as he was the one who asked for the meeting."

"Do you know what he wanted to talk about?" Morgan asked.

"That's the thing. He wasn't sharing much information, though he did seem concerned about the possibility of something nefarious at play in the competition."

"Nefarious? How so?"

"I'm sure I don't know. Now if you'll excuse me, I have to go over tomorrow's schedule."

"Thank you for the information. I'll be in touch."

"Yes, I'm sure you will," Bean said without turning around.

CHAPTER 9

CAL AND MORGAN left the community center and found JJ in the parking lot, standing next to Morgan's truck. "Did you find something?" she asked. "Because if anyone in there knows something, they're certainly not sharing."

"It seems Bean and Sassy have a long, dark history. They started out together in culinary school in the late '70s, but parted ways when Sassy accused Bean of cheating on their final exam."

"How does someone cheat on a baking exam?" Morgan asked.

"Smuggling in special ingredients, perhaps?" Cal said. "Something to make the flavor pop but not enough that the instructor could tell the student was using something unapproved?"

"Well, you did say people call her the Duchess of Spice," Morgan said. "Did they ever prove she cheated?" she asked JJ.

"Not that I could find. Only accusations. She went on to graduate near the top of the class, just behind Sassy."

"And they both went on to have successful careers, albeit, it does seem Sassy *is* the bigger star," Morgan said, drumming her fingers on the hood of her truck. "Perhaps Pierre was threatening to expose Bean's cheating past?"

"I wouldn't think that would be it. The rumors seem to be fairly well known in baking circles," JJ said. "Based on my research, it seems their notorious rivalry has benefited them both."

"Well, the dots seem too vague to connect right now," Morgan said.

"I agree," JJ added.

They both looked at Cal.

"Oh, so now you're seeking my opinion?" Cal asked with a grin. He tapped his finger on his chin. "Well, if this were one of my Detective Philip McDonald books, I would have had Pierre blackmailing the killer which of course means signing his own death warrant."

"Yes, but who would the killer be? Everyone knows Pierre was loyal to Sass. So that nixes her. And everyone knew about Bean's cheating past. What's the motive?" Morgan mused.

JJ held up his phone. "I just ran a quick search. Rumor has it, the Duchess is developing a rival baking show."

"Well, there's your possible motive," Cal said.

"Hannah might have an opinion from a baker's angle, one we're not considering," JJ said. "I'm picking her up. We'll talk about it tonight."

"JJ?"

"Yeah?"

Morgan looked at him meaningfully. "Questions only, okay. You know you're not allowed to reveal anything about the investigation at the moment."

JJ clenched his jaw, started to say something, then turned and walked back into the community center.

"That is one unhappy deputy you have there," Cal said.

"I'm afraid that's not going to change until we solve this case. I don't believe Hannah had anything to do with Pierre's murder, but I can't discount her presence at the crime scene. She found the body." Morgan blew out a breath. "We need to find the killer and clear Hannah once and for all."

MORGAN WALKED into The Perch Mouth Bar and Grille and eased onto a stool at the old carved oak bar.

"Hey, friend," Frankie said as she wiped the counter. "Usual?"

Morgan nodded. One of the nice things about a thirty-year friendship is the other person knew you inside and out.

Frankie pulled a Motor City Mustang Stout from the tap and set it in front of Morgan. "How are you doing? I didn't get a chance to talk to you this morning before Cal showed up and I had to leave. Did you get any sleep last night?"

Morgan took a sip of her beer. Chocolate, coffee, a hint of vanilla. In other words, beer-y goodness. She smiled. "Yeah, some. Thanks again for hanging with me. I couldn't tell you the last time I had a girls night sleep over."

"Sounds fun," Cal said as he slid onto the stool next to Morgan. "I couldn't tell you the last time I had one either."

"Do tell," Frankie said, leaning on the bar. "Would that have been with Amy?

"It was and I don't want to talk about it."

"Sounds like there's a bad-break-up story there," Morgan said. "I'm going to assume it was your fault." She sipped her beer and looked at him out of the corner of her eye. He was staring straight ahead and his jaw was ticking. *Leave it alone for now*, she told herself. *Better switch to teasing mode.* "You know Cal, you're like a bad penny. You seem to turn up everywhere I go."

Cal laughed at that and she felt him relax. "I like to think I'm more of a good luck charm."

"Really? And how is that? Because you're the common link between every murder in Bijoux so far this year," Morgan replied.

Frankie placed a plate of French fries in front of Morgan and a Traverse City cherry hard cider in front of Cal. "I'd say he's more of an albatross." Frankie winked.

"I prefer the high-seas reference." Cal sipped his cider. "Sounds much more wicked than a bad penny. I'll take it." He grinned and jostled her shoulder, then picked up one of Morgan's fries and dipped it into the blob of ketchup she'd squirted onto her plate.

Morgan's stomach did a flip-flop and not from hunger. *Damn. No. Not until I put Ian to rest. But then what…?*

"I tell you I was targeted!" Benny Staples shoved into the bar with some of the other contestants in tow and commandeered three tables. "Sassy's had it out for me ever since we slept together."

Morgan swiveled on her stool and quietly observed the group while Frankie took their drink orders. Benny was definitely a suspect. Maybe he'd say something incriminating after he had a few drinks in him.

"I see you're in stealth mode," Cal whispered.

"Anyone who bursts into a bar, angry and spouting crazy, requires quiet observation in the hopes they'll share information."

"Good point," Cal said, and took a sip of his hard cider.

"Well, it was more than that, wasn't it?" Meg asked. "You two were in love, right? At least that's what I read in the baking chat groups."

"Oh, please. Love has no place in baking beyond the emotion we put into our food." He sneered at her. "Besides, you're just a *home baker*. What would you know?"

"She knows enough to still be in the competition," Paul said. "Face it, you had an off day. Let it go, guy. Nobody likes a sore loser."

"You haven't seen anything yet," Benny said. He took a long swallow of his beer and wiped his mouth with the back of his hand. "Wait until tomorrow. I'm going to expose the queen's entire operation." He looked around the table. "None of you have any idea what's really been going on."

"Enlighten us," Morgan called out from her stool at the bar.

Benny looked up. "You'll have to wait with the rest of them, *Captain Morgan*." He grinned and the bakers giggled. "When I publish my latest blog post."

"Original." Morgan said, getting up and approaching the table. She trained her gaze on him. His eyes skittered away. "Only guilty people look away. You want to tell me about Pierre?"

Benny's nostrils flared, but he didn't respond, only shook his head.

Paul patted him on the back. "He's just blowing off steam, Captain. Really. Benny is grumpy, but harmless. He wouldn't hurt a fly. Well, unless it was in his icing."

MORGAN CLOSED the door to her cottage and dropped onto the couch. She scrolled through her notes on her phone and typed out her to-do list for tomorrow: accelerate research on Benny first thing in the morning, look into Sass and Bean's history and Pierre's possible involvement, figure out why Bean and Pierre were supposed to meet. And probably half a dozen other things she wasn't thinking of at the moment. Griselda jumped onto the back of the sofa and snuggled her head into Morgan's shoulder. Morgan smiled and scratched the cat behind her ears. "I suppose you're wanting some dinner?"

Gris meowed loudly and bolted for the small kitchen, sitting herself beside her bowl. Although Morgan filled Gris's bowl with dry food every morning, she only gave Gris wet food for dinner, a habit the feline would never let her forget.

Morgan filled the food bowl, changed Gris's water, and opened the refrigerator door. The fridge was mostly bare, she'd have to remember to go to the grocery store, but—*thank you Frankie*—there were a few slices of pepperoni pizza leftover from last night. The French fries at the Perch Mouth had barely tied her over. And besides, Cal had eaten most of them. Morgan grabbed the pizza box, a bottle of Mustang Stout, and wandered down the hallway to the spare bedroom. She stood in the doorway for a few moments, staring at the stack of bankers' boxes, fifteen of them. Ian's copies of his case files, photos, and mementos from their life together, a few items of clothing she couldn't bear to part with. She'd gone through everything, multiple times, once she'd healed enough to be able to, and found nothing relative to his case. But since Liz's phone call, she needed to go through everything again. And she couldn't put it off another night.

"Maybe the hundredth time will be the charm," she said to Gris. She placed the pizza carton and beer on the floor. The boxes were all dated according to Ian's years as a detective. Ironically, when she'd left the force she'd transferred all her own former case files onto a USB drive. But Ian had always been old school and preferred paper files. She scanned the room for Box 1. *Ground zero*. There, in the far right corner of the small room, she found it. She carried the box back with her and set it down next the pizza. She sat cross-legged, lifted the cover off, and breathed deeply. His scent—pine mixed with spice— floated out and flooded her senses, as though he were sitting right beside her. She closed her eyes.

Six years on Sunday. She'd look for a way to remember him once the bake-off was over and things were quiet again. Hopefully, she'd have Pierre's murder solved by then, so her mind could be clear and present. "I think we'll go down to the beach Sunday evening, have a fire." She smiled down at Gris, who was watching her intently. "Ian loved the smell of a good fire, you know. Toasted marshmallows, too." She picked up a slice of pizza and took a bite, washed it down with a swig of beer. "Yes. We'll do that. Have a fire, eat some food, pour one out for his memory." She wiped at the tear rolling down her cheek.

A cool breeze went through the room and Morgan shivered. Her phone pinged. It was her stepmom, Zoe. *Just letting you know I'm thinking of you. Hugs.* Morgan shook her head, smiling through her sadness. Besides being the Coffee Cake Queen of Bijoux, Zoe was also the town's resident psychic.

Morgan sighed and started thumbing through the first file in the box in front of her.

CHAPTER 10

MORGAN SAT in her usual booth at Dave's the next morning, rested her arms on the table, and watched the street through the large plate glass window. It was early, 6:30 a.m., the diner was still pretty quiet and there weren't many people out yet, just a few shopkeepers getting ready for the day.

"Good morning. What'll you have this fine morning?" Jerome asked.

Morgan looked up at the waiter. He was smiling. He never smiled. "What's going on? You seem awfully happy."

"What? A guy isn't allowed to be cheery for once in his life?"

"You're not, because you never are." She leaned back. "Spill it."

"For starters, I was happy to hear the horrible Chef Pierre was gone. That man gave me a migraine."

"Speaking ill of the dead, are we?" Cal commented as he slipped into the seat opposite Morgan. "You looked like you could use some company, Captain," he added.

Morgan ignored Cal. "Where were you yesterday morning, between 5 and 6?" she asked Jerome.

Jerome froze. "Here, helping Tom get ready for the morning crowd. Besides, I just meant I'm glad he won't be bothering me anymore. He was quite rude to me with his smoked paprika demands." Jerome pulled out his cell phone and scrolled through his camera roll. "And this. This also makes me happy." He turned his phone around, displaying a picture of a guy who looked a bit like Jerome: thin, dark longish hair, on the short side.

"Your brother?" Morgan asked.

Jerome laughed. "Not likely. My brother is a Marine. This is my new boyfriend, lives over in Grand Pere." He grinned. "I'm not sure yet, but I might be in love. Now what'll you have?"

Morgan smiled back. "I'm happy for you. I'll have a cheese omelet with a blueberry muffin, butter on the side, and a giant black coffee."

"Egg-white omelet. No toast. Whole grain muffin, no butter, and a soy latte, please," Cal ordered.

Morgan stared at him.

"What? I need to stay in fighting form." He patted his stomach.

"Really, is that why you devoured most of my fries yesterday?"

"An aberration."

"French toast with bacon and black coffee for me, please," JJ called out to Jerome as he slid in next to Morgan. He gave Cal the once-over. "The most I've ever seen you fight is with a pen when you couldn't get the cap off."

"It is my lot in life to exist amongst doubters." Cal shook his head. "If you must know, I've started taking self-defense classes over in Lac Voo a couple of months ago. Thought it would help me get into the head of Detective Philip if I worked out throwing punches and dropping bad guys."

"Caleb," Morgan began, "while I think I understand where you're going with this, please remember a few months of classes won't make you indestructible. Don't put yourself in harm's way just because you think you're Iron Man."

"I appreciate your concern, but don't underestimate me, Captain." He looked at her over the rim of his black-framed glasses. "For all you know, I've trained in *Krav Maga* and am merely honing some rusty skills."

"That was awfully specific," JJ said. "You've never mentioned any defense arts before. I call BS."

Cal shrugged. "Think what you will."

"*Krav Maga*?" Morgan snorted. "I'll believe *that* when I see it." She turned to JJ. "So. Anything interesting turn up since we talked late yesterday?"

"Besides the professor's supposed attack skills? No, nothing substantial. It's been a little challenging to find information on the couple of older people involved in the bake-off." He pulled a tablet out of his backpack and clicked it on. "Most of them don't have as deep of an internet presence." He laid the tablet on the table and started scrolling. "Not like the younger bakers who are constantly posting all over social media, as you can see here."

"That makes sense," Morgan said. Jerome arrived with their coffees and she inhaled the amazing scent of roasted and brewed beans and took a sip. *Heaven.* "Cal, tell me about opening night."

"It was pretty typical, I think. The bakers and some of their family members, the crew, Sassy, Damon, Pierre, and Bean of course, were all there. Plenty of sweets and a variety of wines to go with them."

"Did you happen to notice anyone who seemed distracted or angry?"

Cal thought for a moment. He turned to JJ. "Do you remember that Paul guy and Pierre in a little tête-à-tête off to the side? Looked pretty intense."

"Oh yeah. Now that you mention it."

"And neither of you thought anything of this?"

They both shrugged at the same time.

"Really?" Morgan squinted her eyes at them and shook her head. "Okay, we talk to Paul in private after we eat," she said as Jerome arrived with their food.

They were just finishing up and Morgan was ordering a coffee to go when her cell rang. She recognized the ringtone as coming from the station. It was their habit to forward calls to their cells when they weren't at the station She picked it up and answered. "I see. What room number? All right. JJ and I are on our way. Please stay where you are."

"What's up, Cap'n?" JJ asked.

"That was Damon." She exhaled loudly. "He went over to the Firefly to talk to Benny Staples." She met JJ and Cal's eyes. "And found Benny dead. JJ, can you give Doc a call on the way over?"

JJ slid out of the booth and headed to his truck.

Morgan looked at Cal. "I don't suppose I can leave you behind, can I?"

"Not a chance. And I already know the drill," he said as he followed her out the door, "Don't get in the way."

MORGAN PULLED into the Firefly's gravel lot and parked next to JJ. They exited their vehicles and Morgan checked her watch. Almost 7:30 a.m. The sun was up behind them and Lake Michigan's waves rolled and splashed against the sandy shoreline. The air was damp with a slight smell of fish.

"Just so you know, Hannah was with me last night. She was still at my house, feeding Little Dog, when I left to meet you for breakfast," JJ said as they entered the large structure, a former pirate mansion turned bed and breakfast.

"I wasn't going to ask."

"Yes, you were."

"JJ—"

"How *is* Little Dog?" Cal interrupted.

Little Dog was JJ's chihuahua and, next to Hannah, his best friend. "He's cranky, but there seems to be a lot of that going around lately."

Morgan shot JJ a side-eye look, and waved at James the desk clerk as they turned down the hallway to the left. A door was propped open near the end. A sense of déjà vu ran through her. Several of the murders since she'd arrived in Bijoux had somehow ended up connected to the Firefly.

"Wait," Cal said. "Isn't this the same room where Zoe was trapped a couple of months ago?"

"It's the next one down. But, yeah, it all feels eerily familiar, doesn't it?" Morgan walked into the open room. Damon was standing off to the right, near the bed. His heavy black eyeliner was smeared around his eyes and he looked sufficiently shocked. Benny, barefoot and wearing gray sweats, was sprawled on his back on the floor, eyes wide open, staring sightlessly at the ceiling. Morgan's gaze fixed on the uneaten milk chocolate cupcake in his hand. And Hannah's signature wrapper.

"Damon, would you please wait out in the hallway until we're done here? Cal, would you please keep him company?"

"Absolutely," Cal said. He tapped Damon on the arm. "Come on. I'll grab us some coffee from the front desk."

Damon followed Cal out of the room, his head hanging. "Coffee would be just the thing. Thank you."

"Captain," JJ began once they were gone. "The cupcake. It doesn't make sense. There has to be an explanation."

Morgan waved her hand. "We don't know anything, so let's not make assumptions, okay?"

She pulled a pair of nitrile gloves from her back pocket, nodded at JJ and he did the same. Morgan squatted down near the body and studied it, noting the scent of bitter almond. She stood. "We'll need Doc to confirm, but I'm guessing another poisoning. Though I'm not sure of the source this time since it's obvious he didn't eat any of the cupcake."

"Did someone say 'Doc?'" Doc McVie entered the room, pushing a stretcher, his medical bag on top. He paused, tilted his head, adjusted his wire-rimmed glasses, and looked down at Benny. He circled the body before kneeling down and slipping on a pair of gloves. "Definite bitter almond smell. I'll know for sure if it's another cyanide case after I run tox screens and perform the autopsy."

While Doc examined the body, JJ went around the room, snapping pictures. Morgan bagged anything that could be evidence, not that there was much. Benny seemed to travel light. She emptied the small amount of trash from the bathroom receptacle and the one in the main room into the larger sized evidence bags. Hardly anything there of consequence, either. She picked up his coffee cup, sniffed the contents, and winced. "This might be the source," Morgan said. "You got a time of death yet?" she asked Doc McVie.

"Based on body temp, I'd say right around 6 a.m."

"Hey, Captain, look at this." JJ moved Benny's chef jacket to reveal his laptop.

Morgan looked at the screen over JJ's shoulder. A notepad program was open, with one sentence: *I'm sorry.*

"Huh," JJ said. "A possible suicide note? And if so, what could he possibly be sorry enough about to end his life?"

"I ran into Benny last night at the Perch Mouth. He didn't strike me as the type to be apologetic for much of anything. Let's take the computer with us, check for prints. Please run one of your forensic programs and see if you find anything out of the ordinary on the hard drive."

"Roger that," JJ said as he dropped the laptop into a large evidence bag and sealed and dated it.

"Pierre's death. That's likely what he's sorry for," Damon said from the doorway.

Cal followed on Damon's heels.

"It's getting crowded in here," Morgan said. "Let's step out into the hall." A few moments later JJ and Doc wheeled the body out on the stretcher.

"Let me get the exit door," Cal offered, striding ahead of them so they could avoid any commotion in the lobby.

Morgan inclined her head back to Benny's room and they stepped inside. "What do you know, Damon?" Morgan asked, leaning against the open door.

"You witnessed the fiasco at yesterday's judging. Well, Benny left without cleaning up his workspace. That's a big no-no when you're competing. I tried to reach him last night but didn't get an answer." He nodded to the box of evidence bags on the bed. "Check his cell phone, you'll see."

"And you came by this morning to follow up?"

Damon nodded. "I thought I'd try to talk him into getting his things before today's competition started. Sassy was threatening to toss his wares. Bakers spend a lot of money on their tools, and I didn't want to see his investment go to waste."

"How did you get in the room?"

"I knocked. The door was propped open with the security lock, so I let myself in. Found him just as you saw, then I called you."

Cal strode back into the room. "Benny threatened to post a condemning blog last night about Queen Sass and it would appear he did, right around midnight. What did you think of that?" Cal asked.

Damon didn't answer.

Morgan took a step toward Damon. "Where'd he post it?"

"His website blog; has a fair number of followers too," Cal added as he read from his smartphone screen. "Not that we didn't already know this, but he claims he was unhappy about being eliminated in the first round. He goes on to accuse Sassy of plotting against him and ruining his cupcakes when they were on that short snack break before the judging."

"That's all interesting, but he certainly made it sound like he had darker, possibly more damning, information to share. More so than accusations of plots against him," Morgan said. She looked at Damon. "I imagine his post made you angry, though. With his claims aimed at Sassy."

Damon's eyes met hers. They were intense, no longer sad or confused. "No one disrespects Queen Sass on my watch. So yes, I was angry with him."

Morgan watched him carefully, noted the defensive shift in his body language. "Were you mad enough to harm Benny because of what he said? How about Pierre? Was he also disrespectful to Sassy?"

"Wait. I know where you're going with this." Damon held up his hands. "I did not hurt—or kill—anyone. I came by here hoping to convince Benny to take down the blog post. That's it."

"Not to get him to pick up his things, like you told me a few minutes ago?"

"That part is true as well. I was concerned if Sassy threw away his equipment, it'd give him another reason to roast her. I didn't want to see that happen again." He shrugged. "She's delicate. I worry about her."

Morgan tried to reconcile a delicate Sassy with the formidable woman she saw at the bake-off. No, her gut told her Damon was hiding something. "Any additional information you'd like to share?"

"No. Nothing, Captain. May I go now?" Damon checked his watch. "I'm already running behind. I need to get to work."

She motioned toward the lobby. "Go. But don't touch Benny's station." Morgan turned to JJ, who'd just returned from helping Doc. "JJ, please go secure Benny's work area and start going through his things at the community center, see if there's anything notable. I'll be by as soon as I'm done here."

MORGAN SPOTTED Connie standing in the parking lot as she left the Firefly. She turned and started to walk back in. She really was going to have to have it out with Doc. Cal touched her shoulder and she paused.

His eyes danced with humor. "Don't tell me you're going to avoid her? That's not like you."

"You know, I'm getting a little tired of people judging my actions. I'm the police captain. If I don't want to talk to someone, I don't."

Caleb dropped his hand and straightened; his expression no longer friendly. "Sure thing, Captain. Far be it for me to interfere."

"And yet, that's exactly what you do, isn't it?" Morgan knew she shouldn't be angry with him, he hadn't done anything except try to be a friend. She needed sleep, and it still eluded her. *Dammit.* "Cal, look—"

"Well, isn't this cozy," Connie said as she walked onto the large wraparound porch and approached Morgan and Cal. "Am I interrupting something...*important*? Aside from a second murder in as many days, that is."

Morgan gritted her teeth and faced the other woman. "You're running late, Connie. Usually, you show up in time to invade the crime scene."

"Doc and I are taking another distancing break. For the record, it was his idea, not mine." She shook her head. "Honestly, I don't see what his problem is."

"Really?" Morgan shot back. "You eavesdrop on his phone calls then blast it out on the six o'clock news. You violate his privacy and trust. You show up at every crime scene when you know full well you shouldn't be here. Is your career more important than who you step on to get to the top?"

Connie fixed her eyes on Morgan. "It's necessary to share what's going on with the residents of this town. They have a right to know if there's a murderer in our midst." She looked Morgan up and down. "Again."

"I don't have time for this," Morgan said, heading toward her truck, Cal following close behind. "If anything important turns up, you'll be the *first* person I call."

"I know sarcasm when I hear it, Morgan," Connie called out from the porch." I'm not that little girl you used to pick on." Connie called from the porch.

Morgan spun around and strode back to Connie. "Excuse me? I did not pick on you. You picked on me. For years."

"Sure, that's how you'd remember it," Connie sneered. "And don't think I won't use your hoarding of information in my story. I'm going to lead with it. *Bijoux Police Captain fails once again to keep our town safe.* That headline has a nice ring to it."

"I'm not doing this with you again, Connie. Go away. When I know something substantial, I promise either JJ or I will let you know. That's the best I can do right now." Morgan turned and headed for the parking lot.

"I can't believe her nerve," Morgan said to Cal as they both got into the truck.

"What happened between you two?" Cal asked. "I get that Connie is a giant pain, but your dislike of each other goes much deeper."

Morgan rested her forehead on the steering wheel. "I don't like to talk about it, because I still want to respect her privacy."

"Nothing you say will leave here. I give you my word."

"This is dark Bijoux history." Morgan held out her hand and waited until he acknowledged the pinky swear and locked his little finger with hers. "Okay, then. Connie's dad was the town bully. When her mom, Margie, wasn't being used as a punching bag or he wasn't raising hell at the Perch Mouth, Derrick was happy to smack around his only child." Morgan looked at Cal. "Dad got a lot of calls to their house. Margie would never press charges and wouldn't let Connie talk about it. But Connie and I were friends back then, so I knew. I was there one day and witnessed Derrick looking for her, angry because she'd left their back gate open. I stood up to him, got between him and Connie."

"Did you get hurt?"

Morgan shook her head. "No, I think he was smart enough not to mess with the police captain's kid."

"That was brave of you, though."

"I was twelve. What did I know?"

"You knew what it meant to be a friend, and you were trying to help."

"Connie didn't see it that way. Neither did her dad and he went after her once I left. Word got around school about it. She was embarrassed and she blamed me for telling people." Morgan shook her head. "Most everyone already knew because of the bruises on her arms. Bijoux isn't a big town. I swear I never said a single thing to anyone. I even told her that numerous times over the years as we were growing up. But she refused to listen. After I moved away I lost touch with her. Coming back home, even after so many years have passed, well, I guess she still harbors hard feelings."

"What happened to her father?"

"He eventually got arrested for domestic violence—I witnessed Derrick shove Margie and called my dad to come help. Derrick already had two priors—one a barfight and the other, resisting arrest for drunk driving. This was his third offense. He was given the maximum sentence of five years with no time off for good behavior. I thought with her dad gone, Connie would be relieved and let go of her anger toward me." She rasped out a short laugh "Instead, she blamed me for having to grow up without her dad. He apparently left town once he was out of jail, never paid child support so Connie and her mom were always struggling. She was my friend, so I tried to help, share my allowance. It just made things worse. As far as I know, Derrick hasn't had any contact with Connie since." Morgan looked at Cal. He was watching her intently. She could feel his eyes boring into her soul in that way he had, and she wasn't sure how she felt about it. Her stomach frizzled and she shifted her gaze to look out the windshield at the lake. "Connie is complicated."

Cal followed her gaze. "So, I'm learning, is a certain police captain I know."

CHAPTER 11

"Hey, Dad. How are you this morning?"

"You're here early," Able replied without looking up.

"I thought there was a chance Mayor Ed would be here. This seems to be his second office these days."

"Haven't seen him yet today. But it's only 9:30." Able looked up from the cash register. "I know that face. C'mon. There's fresh coffee in the back. Some cookies, too." He wrapped his arm around her shoulders. "What's going on that has you so upset on a weekend when you should be relaxing?"

"Coffee first, please." Morgan followed her dad to the back of the store. She accepted the hot beverage, smiling gratefully. She took a sip. Hot and strong. *Perfect*. "Where's Zoe?"

"She's in the back, getting ready to run over to Hannah's bakery. She's been helping out there since Hannah's been in the competition. And you're changing the subject."

"Did I hear my name?" Zoe asked as she walked up and stood next to Able. She was wearing a flowy dark burgundy dress which perfectly complemented her silver hair. "You look like you could use a hug," she said to Morgan.

"No, I'm fine," Morgan said, but she realized she must've been far from convincing when Zoe bounded around the coffee bar and embraced her. Morgan stiffened, then relaxed. Zoe smelled like lavender and it was soothing. "I was wrong. That was nice. Thank you."

"I don't think I've ever heard her say that," Cal said, walking up to them.

"That she's wrong?" Able handed him a cup of coffee and a shortbread cookie dipped in chocolate and rolled in nuts. "It does not happen often. Best to make a note of the day and time."

Morgan shot him an annoyed glance. Cal seemed to always show up out of nowhere. "Didn't I just drop you off at the Raven's Nest?" Morgan asked, frowning. "How does your store make any money with you never being there?"

"For starters, I don't open until 10. Secondly, I knew there'd be coffee already made here. With the way the day started, I was looking for an immediate infusion." Cal held up the cookie. "Expanding your repertoire?" he asked Zoe.

Morgan felt Zoe go slack and, before she could react, Able was already helping his wife into a chair. "What's going on?" Able asked her. "What do you see, hon?"

Zoe motioned for Morgan. Morgan leaned over and Zoe touched her cheek. "Ian. He's here." She shuddered and her voice deepened. "I know you won't stop until you have all the answers. But you're asking all the wrong questions. The truth is right in front of you. Be careful Fay. Promise me you'll be careful...."

Fay. Ian always called her by her middle name. While Morgan didn't believe in psychics, she had to admit her stepmom came up with some interesting information from time to time and was more right than wrong when it came to her 'premonitions.' And what she just said did send a shiver through Morgan. *I'll just keep the peace and go along.* "Okay. Sure. I promise I'll be careful."

Zoe's hand dropped. Cal handed her a bottle of water from the nearby cooler. She took a long drink, steadied herself, then smiled. "Well, I need to get over to Hannah's Heavenly Confections."

"Are you sure you don't want to lie down for a while?" Able said. "I can run over and leave a note on the door telling customers to come back later. You're still looking a bit pale."

"No, thank you. The fresh lake air will do me good." Zoe pushed up from the folding chair. "Besides, Hannah is counting on me." Zoe gave each of them a quick hug and left.

Morgan considered what Zoe had just said. "If Hannah's bakery has been open during the bake-off, it might offer an explanation why her cupcakes were at both crime scenes. Besides the obvious one that

Hannah herself placed them there." She stopped, looked at her dad. "There was another murder. Or suicide. Benny Staples. I'm waiting for Doc McVie to confirm one way or another. Please don't repeat that last piece of information."

Able nodded. "Of course. I won't say a word. How's JJ handling Hannah being a suspect?"

"Horribly, as you can imagine. But he's keeping his head for the most part. In spite of the cupcakes, I place her at the bottom of the list, anyway."

"Especially so since it sounds like your suspect pool just got a lot larger. With the bakery open, her cupcakes could have been purchased by anyone."

"You're right." She paused. "I'm annoyed with myself it didn't even occur to me Hannah might keep the shop open right now."

"By the way, you didn't fuss about Zoe's premonition, like you usually do," Able said. "And normally you would have already asked Hannah about the bakery."

Cal leaned on the counter and took a sip of coffee. "Morgan hasn't been sleeping. It's been worrisome, to be honest."

Able arched an eyebrow.

"I may have mentioned I've been having trouble sleeping to JJ and Mr. Know-it-All over here." Morgan threw Cal a look she hoped said butt out. Not that he would comply.. "I'm fine. My deputy and my supposed friend here have an overactive imagination lately when it comes to me."

"Morgan, talk to your old man." Able gestured to the chair Zoe had vacated and Morgan sat down. Able pulled up a stool and sat across from her. Able might be her dad, but he'd always be a cop first, and she knew from experience it did no good to argue with those instincts. "Fine. What Cal said. I'm not sleeping very well. I've been dreaming quite a bit about Ian lately. It'll be six years on Sunday, well, tomorrow, since he died."

Cal touched her arm. "I'm so sorry. I didn't realize."

"Why would you? It's not something I like to talk about, if you hadn't noticed."

"There's more though, isn't there?" Able asked.

Might as well get it all out. Maybe saying the words out loud would give her another perspective. "Liz called. An old informant of ours told her Ian's partner, James Wheat…" She paused and took a deep, shaky breath. "The informant is claiming James murdered Ian."

"Wheat?" Able frowned. "He was Ian's best friend."

"I know Dad. He was my friend too. We trusted James with our lives."

"He wouldn't be the first cop to turn dirty," Cal added.

"No, but it's still overwhelming to process. We're taking the information with a grain of salt, but Liz thought she'd go ahead, follow up, and contact James. Unfortunately, near as we can tell, he moved to the Caribbean after retirement the end of last year." She glanced over at Cal. "You asked about Frankie. Liz let her know what was up and she came and stayed the night with me."

Cal nodded. "Frankie is a good human."

"That she is. One of my favorites."

Able crossed his arms. "And what does your gut tell you about this information?"

She ran a hand through her hair. "James was our friend, but my instincts tell me it could be true. Liz asked me to go through Ian's things again, see if I missed any potential evidence he may have been collecting against James."

"I take it you haven't found anything so far?" Able asked.

Morgan shook her head. "No. But I just started last night. This bake-off case is taking most of my time right now, as it should."

"What are you doing tonight?" Cal asked.

"Eating the last piece of leftover pizza and going through another box. Why?"

"How about I bring over lasagna from the Italian place in Lac Voo? I'll pick it up after my self-defense class." His eyes met hers. "And I'll help you go through the boxes."

Morgan's breath caught. Letting Cal go through Ian's things felt awfully intimate, maybe even invasive. But he did have a way of seeing things differently than her. Maybe, just maybe, he'd find something she missed. That alone would be worth any awkwardness she might be feeling. "Okay. Thank you. And you might want to bring some wine with that lasagna, I'm fresh out." She rolled her neck and stood. "Back to work. I have bakers to question."

Cal just stood there, looking at her.

"What? Do you need to come with me for some weird Caleb reason?"

"Actually, I was heading over to the community center to set up Sassy's cookbook signing in the old library. I dropped the books off yesterday."

"Fine, you can ride with me. Try not to get anyone killed at this signing, though, okay? Or Mayor Ed is liable to run you out of town."

CHAPTER 12

"HEY, HANNAH, DO YOU HAVE A MOMENT?" Morgan asked as she approached Hannah's baking station.

Hannah wiped her hands on her apron and glanced at the large gym clock. "Sure, they won't start the judging until later. Damon told us about Benny. It's just horrible."

Morgan motioned for the younger woman to follow her to the bleachers. Hannah sat down, but Morgan stood in front of her, composing her thoughts.

"Morgan? I don't have a lot of time. How about we just get to whatever it is you'd like to know?"

"Absolutely." Morgan sat down next to Hannah. "What's your experience with Benny Staples?"

"Not much. I knew about him because of being in the business. He's volatile. He and Queen Sass have a history, not a long one, but a history just the same. They were an item a few years back."

"Any idea how it ended?"

Hannah thought for a moment. "My memory is she broke it off with him. He had ambitions to take over her empire, I think. She had other ideas."

"How about Pierre?"

Hannah teared up, wiped at her eyes with the heel of her hand. "I still can't believe one of my cupcakes killed him."

"We're fairly certain your cupcake was just the delivery system. Someone had to put the cyanide inside of it. So, what do you know about Pierre?"

"I've only known him in the context of this event, but he was always professional. Not mean, just firm about his expectations of us bakers."

"I thought Damon was your wrangler for the show."

"He is, but Pierre mentored us, went over flavors and our recipes." Hannah chuckled through her tears. "Can't have us poisoning the judges!" She clapped a hand over her mouth. "I can't believe I just said that."

Morgan cracked a smile. "No worries. Do you know if anyone had a problem with him reviewing their recipes?"

"Come to think of it, he and Paul had a pretty heated conversation. No idea if it was about that, though." Hannah rubbed the back of her neck. "Is any of this helpful?"

"Maybe. Potentially. I never know what pieces might come together to solve the puzzle, so I collect as many as I can." Morgan's phone pinged and she glanced at the text. "JJ's on his way. How are things going with him?"

Hannah shook her head. "I've known JJ since high school. We've always been good friends but never dated. I mean, he was just… always there, you know? When I needed a shoulder. In senior year, when I found out my boyfriend was cheating on me, JJ was there for me. He's a good listener and always made me laugh. From then on we became good friends. But we never dated or anything. I had boyfriends in college, and he dated a girl over in Lac Voo for a while until she got a job offer in Seattle. She promised him they would do the long-distance thing, but she ended up ghosting him. And then I became JJ's shoulder. I was single at the time…and eventually it just became obvious to us both and we started dating." Hannah sighed. "We got into a comfortable routine. But in the past few months, JJ's been different—overprotective, vigilant almost…"

Morgan saw the strain in Hannah's eyes and wondered if the stress of the recent spate of murders had triggered something in JJ that hadn't been there before. Bijoux had always been a town with a low crime-rate. Murder-free for almost a century… Should she have a talk with JJ? Maybe he could benefit from seeing a therapist. But how could she bring that up?

"…and now since Pierre's murder," Hannah went on, "he's been making me crazy. I had no idea he had such an overprotective streak. I mean, he practically ordered me not to talk to you about the case unless either he or a lawyer was present. Can you believe that?" Hannah shook her head. "Maybe JJ and I just aren't meant to be. Maybe we should have just stayed friends."

Morgan touched Hannah's hand and offered a smile. "You don't have to make any decisions today. Wait until you're not under so much stress."

Hannah nodded. "Yeah, I guess you're right. This has been an intense weekend."

"I really appreciate you talking to me anyway, despite JJ's warning."

"I didn't do anything wrong, so what is there to hide?"

"Agreed. One more question, do you know if Paul had a problem with Benny?"

"Honestly, everyone had a problem with Benny. The man was not likable."

"Bakers!" Damon called out from the front of the gym. "Please return to your stations."

"Thank you, Morgan." Hannah stood. "Fingers crossed I get through today and into the finals. That $10,000 prize money would help me get a start on fixing up the bakery. I'd love to make the kitchen more efficient, replace all the storage, and make room for a helper."

Morgan smiled. "Fingers *and* toes. But not that you need it. You'll do great."

CHAPTER 13

"Looks good in here," Morgan said, picking up a copy of *Queen Sass Dishes*. Cal had clearly gone to considerable effort setting up the book signing in the former grade-school library. The colorful display featured a life-sized cut-out of Queen Sass herself and hundreds of copies of the new book, along with a selection of her previous releases. "What time is the signing?" Morgan asked.

"At one." Cal checked his watch. "I'm almost done here. Just need to put out some bottled water, then I'm heading back to the Raven's Nest to get Henry situated."

Morgan nodded, noting the room still looked like a library with its wall-to-wall sturdy oak shelves and old-fashioned card-catalog. The Bijou Community Center Committee had recently turned it into a retro hang out, with plans to hold the Bijoux Book Club monthly meetings there. They'd even installed a coffee bar, a bakery display case, and several bistro-style tables and chairs.

"Boy, this place sure has changed," JJ said from the doorway. "I remember having to sit in here and write '*I will be quiet*' a thousand times while the librarian watched me like a hawk from her desk." He rubbed his hand, as if it cramped with the memory. "Anyway, I ran into Mayor Ed as I was leaving the station, Captain. I didn't figure you'd mind if I filled him in on our latest situation."

"Not at all. Thanks for dealing with that," Morgan replied, happy to have avoided the confrontation, though she knew there'd be one eventually.

"We also got Doc's report in. Definitely cyanide. No way to know if it was suicide or not. At least for now."

"Cal and I saw Benny last night at the Perch Mouth. He certainly didn't talk like someone who was depressed. Or sorry. Exactly the opposite, as a matter of fact."

"The man had a definite axe to grind," Cal said as he lined up water bottles, then gave the books one last straightening. "He was angry and bitter and made a point of letting everyone know it."

"I'm still going through his computer, so maybe something will turn up that'll help us," JJ said. "Interestingly, though, there were no fingerprints on the keys or anywhere else on the laptop."

Morgan turned to him. "Really. Not even Benny's?"

JJ shook his head. "Nope. Wiped clean."

"I'd say that likely rules out suicide, then. It wouldn't make any sense for Benny to take the time to wipe down his own keyboard before or after ingesting cyanide." She started pacing. "Based on that theory, whoever poisoned him would definitely want to eliminate any evidence of having been there or writing the suicide note." Morgan stopped and leaned against the coffee bar. "I'm waiting to talk to Paul at the next break, but Hannah did corroborate what both you and Cal said about their fight."

JJ straightened. "When did you talk to Hannah?"

"Just before you got here. I wanted her take on Benny and Pierre."

"And that's all it was?"

"Look, JJ, if I thought Hannah was guilty, I would have arrested her by now. Or, at the very least, hauled her in for deeper questioning. I happen to think she's not, but I can't go on my gut with that." She frowned at him. "We have to establish evidence that clears her. You know that."

JJ slumped. "I know, I know."

"Do you trust me?"

"Of course, I do."

"Then let's do our job and figure this out so we can all move on." Moving on seemed to be her theme this week. She glanced at Cal, who was watching her intently. "What?"

"I'm wondering who your suspects are. It's an unusual situation."

"Every murder in this town is unusual." Morgan shook her head. "Having said that, we have high stress conditions, volatile personalities, and a bunch of bakers with interconnected pasts."

"Not to mention the stakes are high with a possible TV show on the line," Cal added.

"It's true," JJ said. "I did some digging. Sassy is developing a new series based on everyday home baking. Whatever that means, but that's what I read."

"Who do you like for Pierre's murder?" Cal asked Morgan.

"Well, I did like Benny. Given his issues with Sassy, maybe he wanted to get even with her and take out her sous chef, thinking it might hobble the show."

"That would be devilish," Cal said. "Definitely would carry the possibility of shutting down the production, though that obviously didn't happen."

"Devilish?" JJ and Morgan said it at the same time.

"Jinx," JJ added. "You'll have to buy me a Coke."

Morgan smiled at JJ. "You got it. I still need to talk to Paul. Since he was fighting with Pierre, we need to figure out what that was about. Then there's Bean—Pierre was supposed to meet with her right before he was killed. I talked to her, but she claims Pierre never showed up." She nodded to JJ. "As soon as the show breaks for the book signing, I'll talk to Paul. Would you please hang out here and keep your eye on things?"

"Will do, Captain." He poured himself a cup of coffee and plunked himself down onto one of the stools. The cupcakes left over from the morning's bake were on a tiered stand at the end of the counter. JJ grabbed one, and peeled back the liner, looked it over, then set it down on the counter. "Um, maybe not today."

"BAKERS, please move your trays to the end of your station," Damon instructed. "Sassy and Bean will be visiting with each of you to judge this morning's creations."

Morgan watched the interactions intently from her spot beside the door leading to the cafeteria. Sassy and Bean stood stiffly apart and their body language told her they weren't entirely comfortable with each other this morning, though they were friendly with the bakers. The duo made their way to the front of the judging dais.

"Well done, bakers," Sassy said. "I know this morning has not been an easy one for you as we've continued to mourn the loss of Pierre and now Benny as well." Bean patted her on the back. Sassy squared her shoulders. "But the show must go on. Now, it's time to taste your bakes. Hannah, please bring your tray of cinnamon cakes up here and tell us about your inspiration."

Hannah placed her arrangement of twenty-four cakes on the judging table. "My boyfriend loves cinnamon candies, so I included crushed ones in the buttercream frosting for some added crunch. He was my inspiration for this round."

Bean and Sassy each took a bite. "Oh. Oh my," Sassy said. "That is spicy." She took a sip of water.

Hannah frowned. "I'm so sorry. Is it too much?"

Bean waved her hand. "Not at all, just an unexpected surprise. I quite like it."

"As do I," Sassy added. "Quite scrummy. You may return to your station."

The remaining four bakers each followed and presented their trays. "Really, Paul, you've out done yourself with the addition of smoked pork to your cinnamon cake," Sassy said.

"Highly unexpected," Bean added.

"Indeed. And in a good way." Sassy surveyed the bakers. "The stakes are high for your final bake today. And it will determine who will go onto the finals tomorrow. Your challenge is to create a cupcake tower."

"Forty-eight cupcakes in total using three signature flavors," Bean added. "Sixteen of each flavor and all must be decorated exquisitely, taste delicious, and be assembled to perfection." She stared at each baker. "No. Wobbly. Towers."

"Damon will be on hand to assist should you need anything," Sassy said with a smile. "Bean as well. I will be in the library for my book signing for the next hour or so. And yes, I've saved a signed copy of *Queen Sass Dishes* for each of you."

Damon stepped forward. "Ready Bakers? You have three hours to complete this task. On your marks! Start baking!"

The bakers all scrambled back to their stations and began assembling ingredients. Morgan stopped Sassy as she walked by on her way to the library. "A word, please."

"I don't have time. Make an appointment with Damon," she huffed and kept walking.

Morgan fell into step alongside her. "Look, I know this has been a stressful time for you, but I need to ask you about Pierre. It will only take a moment."

Sassy sighed, stopped walking, and turned to Morgan. "What? What could you possibly want to know about Pierre?"

"You and he were friends, correct? Did he confide in you?"

"Yes, we were friends. And on occasion, usually over a nice scotch at the end of the day, we might have confided in each other." The older woman squinted at Morgan. "Are you going somewhere with this, Captain? We did not have *that* sort of relationship, if that's what you're implying. Truly, simply good friends. And yes, if you're wondering, I miss him terribly."

"Do you know why he wanted to talk to Bean the morning he was killed?"

"What did Bean say about it?"

"She said he didn't show up."

Morgan watched Sassy's expression shutter. "Well, I certainly have no idea. Now, I must get to the signing. My fans await." She gestured toward the front door where people were lined up from the library entry and on outside the building.

Morgan nodded. "If you think of any reason why he may have wanted to talk to her, please let me know."

Sassy walked away without responding. *The Queen is definitely hiding something.*

Morgan returned to the gym and made her way toward Paul. The assistant director stepped in front of her, blocking her path. "We're filming. You need to wait over there." She pointed to the side of the gym near the doors to the cafeteria.

Morgan frowned and strode over to the bleachers, and plunked down on the bench in the front row. When the director yelled cut,

Morgan took advantage of the break in the competition as the second camera man began shooting what the director had called "cutaways." She approached Paul, who was busy tidying up his workstation.

He glanced up at Morgan, but his focus was on his work. "Can't talk now," he said. "If you haven't noticed, we're in the middle of a competition."

Damon approached, carrying a tablet. "Captain Morgan, may we do this later. Things are highly stressful right now."

"Yes," she said. "They are." She turned to Paul. "And this will only take a minute, then you can get back to your filming. Tell me, why were you arguing with Pierre the night before he died?"

Paul dropped the spatula he was using the scrape the bowl in his hand clean and it clattered to the floor. He picked it up and set in the sink, then grabbed a clean one from the dishrack. "Nothing important."

"Humor me."

Paul sighed. "Butter. We were disagreeing about butter." He placed the bowl in the sink with some dish soap and turned on the water. "I prefer salted organic. Pierre had reviewed my recipe and suggested I might want to change it. He, no surprise, believes European is the best." He started washing his dishes. "Well, *believed*. That's it. Nothing more."

"Butter is a highly contested item in the baking world," Damon said. "Salted, unsalted. European, organic. The list goes on."

Morgan's left eye twitched and she rubbed it. If she didn't link a suspect to the murders soon, the competition would be over and all the potential suspects would be gone. Not that she had any strong suspects at this point, beyond Sassy and possibly Bean, though they were near the bottom alongside Hannah. And assuming Paul was being truthful about the whole butter thing, that removed him from the list. The investigation was sinking like a soufflé after a door slam.

CHAPTER 14

"Looks like the signing is going well," Morgan said to JJ as she sat on the stool next to him. "Anything suspicious?"

JJ laughed. "Only if you consider the fact that this many people need an autographed cookbook." He shook his head. "I had no idea baking was this popular in Bijoux."

Morgan smiled. "Maybe you should pay more attention to your girlfriend."

JJ grew serious. "Yeah, she might not be that—my girlfriend—much longer. She's pretty mad at me."

"I'm sorry to hear that." She patted his arm. "I'm sure she'll come around. Maybe give her a little space until the bake-off is over. There's a lot of stress in that room."

"No cutters! Get to the back of the line!"

Morgan glanced at the long line-up and spotted the usually irate Mr. Dominic, holding his cane across the door, barring a lanky young man, about six-feet-tall with dark hair and glasses, from getting in.

"I see Mr. Dominic has declared himself the official *line* police in Bijoux," Morgan whispered to JJ.

"Maybe he thinks they'll be serving free coffee cake here, too," JJ whispered back.

The young man held up his hands. "Not cutting. Honest. Just checking on the book supply."

Morgan strode to the door and called out, "It's okay, Mr. Dominic. He's only here to make sure things are running smoothly."

Mr. Dominic reluctantly lowered his cane but continued to glower at the other man.

"You must be Cal's nephew." Morgan held out her hand. "Morgan Hart."

"Right. The police captain." He shook her hand. "And guilty as charged. Henry Joseph, said nephew." He grinned. "Do you like what I did there?"

JJ, who'd followed Morgan, uttered a groan. "You really are related to the professor."

"And you must be JJ. Uncle Cal has told me all about both of you."

"Yeah, well, don't believe most of it," Morgan said.

Henry laughed. "If you'll excuse me, I need to check on the signing, make sure Queen Sass has everything she needs."

"He's like a mini-Cal," Morgan whispered to JJ. "How spooky is that?"

WITH THE SIGNING over and the final judging not for another hour, Morgan and JJ headed back to the station. JJ's computer was beeping, and he rushed over to check it.

"Whatcha got?" Morgan asked. She sat at her desk and reached for Bubbles, the blonde Powerpuff Girl action figure, and began tossing her in the air. Bubbles helped her think.

"A diagnostic I was running on Benny's laptop shows a block of data was deleted around the same time he died." He hit a couple of keys and leaned back in his chair. "I just told the program to recover the data. It might take a couple of hours, though. Maybe longer, depending on how much is actually there and the type of data it is."

The station door chimed and Sassy walked in. "I only have a few moments, but I'm concerned about the question you asked me regarding Pierre and Bean." She wrung her hands together. "I couldn't stop thinking about it all through the book signing. I believe they may have been plotting against me."

"In what way?" Morgan asked. She stood. "And to what end?"

"You've likely heard the rumors about a new home baking show I have in the works? Bean has a similar idea. She thinks I stole it. I'm beginning to believe Pierre may have leaked it to her before speculation began in the press."

"Why would you think that?"

Sassy glanced nervously around the room. She leaned in and whispered, "I think they were having an affair." She straightened and crossed her arms over her chest. "Neither of them have spoken about being together, but I saw how they looked at each other when they thought I wasn't looking. All googly-eyed, if you get my meaning."

Morgan considered Sassy's words. "Do you believe this had something to do with his death?"

"Oh, well, I couldn't say for certain now, could I?" Morgan watched Sassy shut down again. "But it is one's civic duty to speak up isn't it? Now, I have a judging to get to. If you'll excuse me." She spun on her heel and left.

Morgan turned to JJ. "I'm going to assume she doesn't realize this information makes her a suspect."

"I'd have to agree. Though, if she did, why incriminate herself? That makes no sense, either."

"I want it stopped!" Mr. Dominic announced loudly from the station door. He walked to the counter and pounded his cane on it. "It goes against all things natural!" He teetered and the seventy-something woman with him—with an equally bad hair dye job of black instead of red—steadied him.

"What's going on, Mr. Dominic?" Morgan asked. She looked at the woman. "And you are—?"

"Audrey Burns. Augustus is my BF. That's short for boyfriend. We met at the Lac Voo Bingo Hall and it was love at first sight. I'm here to represent his issue." She smiled, her mouth tight. "I used to be a lawyer over in Lac Voo before I retired."

Morgan's eyes narrowed. "And just what would that issue be?"

"The complete disregard by some people in this town for law and order," Mr. Dominic replied.

"Excuse me?"

"It's true. This town is basically lawless with the way people cut in and out of lines. They pay no attention to societal conventions." Audrey patted Mr. Dominic's arm. "It's very upsetting for Auggie. His doctor says it's affecting his blood pressure."

Morgan considered Mr. Dominic. *Auggie?* "Mr. Dominic, while cutting a line is rude, it's not illegal. I suggest you relax and not let such things bother you."

"I knew you'd say that," Mr. Dominic countered. "I guess I'll be taking matters into my own hands." He brandished his cane in the air.

"Oh, darling, we don't want to hurt anybody now, do we?" Audrey said.

"Damn skippy I want to hurt someone. You don't get to be as old as I am and not have a bad attitude about some things. Like line cutting."

"I'll tell you what, Mr. Dominic," Morgan began. "You're still a volunteer deputy, right? How about you monitor situations and let JJ here know when something disturbing happens. That way, you don't have to get involved. Or angry. That should help your blood pressure."

"Um, do I have a say in this?" JJ asked from his desk.

Morgan winked at him but was careful to make sure neither Mr. Dominic nor Audrey could see her. "Just for the time being, JJ, until things settle down."

"Ah, gotcha. Okay. Mr. Dominic, I'm your man."

"There now. That wasn't so difficult, was it?" Audrey said. She slipped an arm around Mr. Dominic and he leaned against her. "Is this agreeable to you, Auggie?"

"It is. Now let's go keep an eye on that book signing line over at the community center," he said as they left. "You'll be hearing from me, deputy."

Morgan and JJ looked at each other and shook their heads. She checked her watch. "It is almost time for the judging. You want to head over to the center with me and watch Hannah get into the finals?"

"I absolutely believe she'll get in, but I think I'll stay here and keep an eye on the laptop."

"JJ…" Morgan began.

He shook his head and sighed. "I've been thinking about what you said. Maybe you're right and I should give her some time and space. I don't want to add to the stress she's already feeling."

Morgan walked around to his desk and waited for him to look at her. When he finally did, she said, "I can tell you from experience, not being there will be even more stressful for you. Besides, I haven't known you to back down from a difficult situation yet. The data recovery isn't going to go any faster with you staring at it."

"All right, Captain." He pushed up from his desk. "If Hannah gets mad, I'm telling her it was your idea."

Morgan laughed. "Fair enough."

CHAPTER 15

"EVERYONE. Please take a breather while we get your workspaces cleaned up in preparation for today's final judging," Damon said to the bakers. They glanced nervously around at each other, then filed out to the cafeteria where Elise was waiting with a large basket of wedge-cut French fries. Morgan and JJ followed from where they'd been sitting on the bleachers.

"French fries?" Morgan asked Elise.

"I was thinking it would help counteract all the sweetness they've been indulging in today. You know, they have to taste everything they make to determine if the flavors are there. I thought something salty would be a nice palate cleanser."

"Mom's right," Hannah said, grabbing one of the wedges and avoiding JJ's eyes. Steven set a platter of cheese and crackers out along with glasses of iced tea. The bakers filled their plates and stuffed their mouths.

Morgan's stomach growled. *Shush. We have to save ourselves for lasagna later tonight.* Though she did grab a slice of cheese.

"I'm just so nervous," Meg said. "I've never gotten this far in any of the competitions I've been in."

"It's obvious you've been practicing and deserve to be here just as much as the rest of us," Paul said.

Meg frowned. "That's not what you said in the beginning, when Benny was criticizing me."

"I was obviously wrong," Paul admitted. "And the judges have been happy with your bakes. Can't argue against that."

Morgan noted the skeptical glances the other four bakers shared. "How many times have you competed?" she asked Meg.

"Oh. Well. Almost more than I can count." She thought for a moment. "Twelve, I think. Maybe fifteen. It's my passion."

"And you never made it past the first round?" Morgan asked.

"No, this is the first time for me. Benny was right about me." She glanced at Paul. "Paul, too. My food was always pretty, now it tastes good, too. I've managed to add substance to my style." She smiled and sipped her glass of tea. "I really need this."

Morgan tilted her head. "How so?"

"Her ego was in the gutter," Paul answered. "I've known Meg here for a while now and she was ready to give up. This was going to be her last competition."

"But who knows now?" Meg added. "If I make it past today, maybe I'll keep competing. I could use a win for once."

"At least you won't have to worry about Benny dogging you," Paul said. He looked at Morgan. "As you saw, he did not like Meg."

"Not that he liked any of us all that much." Hannah added.

"He had an issue with bakers who weren't professionally trained," Paul explained. "He had zero respect for home bakers and often criticized them in his blog."

"So, you're not sad he's gone, either," Morgan stated.

Paul wiped his mouth with a napkin and dropped it on his plate. "Of course not. And I don't believe you'll find one person here who is."

"I completely concur," another baker, about forty-five with a buzz cut, said. "I couldn't stand the guy, either."

"And your name is?" Morgan asked.

"Bobby. Bobby the Baker. Alliteration is my thing. All my creations are alliterative."

"I agree with Bobby and Paul," said the thirty-something brunette sitting across the table from Morgan. "Benny wasn't a nice person. And I'm Eva, which I'm sure you're getting ready to ask."

Morgan looked around the table and silently added four suspects to her list; five if she were to count Hannah, which she wasn't ready to do. Well, to Benny's list anyway. She was still looking for a link to Pierre's murder.

"What about Pierre?" Morgan asked.

"What about Pierre?" Meg repeated.

"What did all of you think about him?"

"What I told you earlier," Hannah said. "We all have—had—nothing but respect for him."

"Other than his choices when it came to butter," Paul added with a smirk.

"It's to be expected," Eva said. "He was European, after all. He was always going to go with what he knows and try to get us to follow suit."

Morgan noted the baker's nametag. "Did you know Pierre well, Eva?"

Eva shrugged. "I was on an earlier season of this show and met him then. He was fine to work with, just opinionated. It's a show requirement we bring original recipes and Pierre goes through them with us. Advises where he sees an issue and offers suggestions."

"Suggestions?" Bobby snorted. "More like diva-ish demands."

"Did he take issue with anyone's recipes?" JJ asked, addressing the group.

Before the bakers could respond, Damon called out from the doorway, "Bakers, Queen Sass and the Duchess of Spice are ready to discuss your bakes. Please return to your stations." He frowned at Morgan and JJ. "Now, if you don't mind."

The bakers filed into the gym and took their places at their work areas. Sassy and Bean were standing behind the dais and Damon stood off to the side, while the director of photography moved in for a series of hand-held camera close-ups. "As you know, we will eliminate two bakers today," Sassy began, "which means only three of you will go onto tomorrow's final bake. Good luck to each and every one of you." She smiled. "Paul, please bring up your tower of cupcakes."

Paul approached the large front table and gently placed the tower of forty-eight cupcakes in front of the judges.

"Tell us about your bakes," Bean said.

"I'm from Michigan's Upper Peninsula, so I took my inspiration from the pine forests. Therefore, I have these arranged my tower in the shape of a conifer. I used a vanilla sponge base, filled with cherry mascarpone cream, drizzled with a gin reduction to bring out the pine scent and flavor."

Sassy cut one of the cupcakes in half and she and Bean each took a bite. They were silent for a moment and Morgan saw sweat beading on Paul's forehead. Never would she have imagined baking to be so competitive.

"Simply delicious," Sassy declared. "The flavors are beautiful."

"I was worried it would taste like a pine tree," Bean added. The bakers giggled and Paul smiled nervously. "I was wrong. Quite lovely."

Paul thanked the judges and took his tower back to his workstation.

"Hannah. Please present your bake," Bean said.

Hannah glanced at JJ and Morgan as she carried her tower of glittery magenta cupcakes to the judging table. "My inspiration is Bijoux, which is French for jewel. So, what I've made for you today uses a lemon cake sponge base with lime curd filling and raspberry French meringue frosting. And, as you can see, I've dusted them with edible glitter to bring out the jewel theme."

"This is just so very pretty, Hannah," Sassy said. She looked up. "You have a definite gift for presentation. Now, let's see what they taste like."

"Nice even bake. The flavors come through, but they're not overpowering. This is the best bite of the day of all the bakes so far," Bean said.

"Wow. Thank you," Hannah said. She looked over at JJ and Morgan, who gave both gave her a thumbs up.

As the last of the bakers finished presenting their cupcake towers, Sassy and Bean, along with Damon, conferred off to the side, occasionally glancing at the bakers while they talked. After several minutes, the trio took their places in front of the judging table.

"As much as we'd like to take all of you along to the final, it's just not possible," Damon said.

"You've all done well today, though some of your towers were wobbly and some flavors were a touch on the bland side," Sassy said, folding her hands in front of her. "I want to personally thank all of you for participating in this weekend's bake-off. Now, to the part you've all been waiting for. The winner of today's competition is, once again, Paul. Paul, we loved your original pine flavors. Please step forward."

"And I quite enjoyed the gin," Bean added with a wink.

"Second place goes to Bijoux's own baker, the one whose winning entry brought us here to this lovely town in the first place. Hannah, please step forward."

Sassy surveyed the three remaining bakers. "As you know, there's only space for one more. And that baker is someone who has surprised us all this weekend. Meg, will you please join Paul and Hannah?"

Eva and Bobby, though obviously disappointed, clapped and congratulated the three finalists. The director yelled cut for lunch and the crew raced over to the bakers' stations and snatched up a cupcakes on their way to the cafeteria.

Morgan and JJ rushed over to Hannah. "You made it!" JJ went in for a hug, but Hannah held back.

"People will see us. I'd like to keep things professional. How would it look if I'm seen hugging one of the investigators in the murder investigation?"

Morgan watched JJ's smile droop.

"Of course," he said, and stepped back.

"I knew you'd make it to the next round!" Morgan grinned.

"Thank you. I really appreciate your faith in me." Hannah smiled at Morgan, but avoided looking at JJ. "If you don't mind, I'm exhausted and need to get some rest. Tomorrow is going to be intense."

"I'll take you home," JJ said.

Hannah set her mouth in a firm line. "I have my car here, but thanks anyway. I'll see you later."

JJ stared after his girlfriend. Morgan put a hand on his shoulder. "This entire situation is stressful, but I have faith in the two of you. I just want you to know that."

"I wish I did." JJ sighed. "I'm going to run over to the station and check on the data recovery. Unless you need me for anything else?"

"Thanks, and while you're there, can you do a background check on Bobby and Eva too? I just want to rule them out," Morgan said. "I have a cat to feed and some boxes to go through. Let me know if you find anything. And make sure you get some rest, too."

"Roger that, Captain. Have a good night."

CHAPTER 10

"I KNOW, I KNOW," Morgan said as she walked into her cottage and dropped her keys on the small table near the front door. Griselda stood on the kitchen counter, meowing nonstop. Morgan shook her head as she approached the cat. "You know you're not allowed up there, I don't care if it is dinnertime," she said. She scooped Gris up, gave her a snuggle, then placed her gently on the wood plank floor.

"What have you been up to today?" She dished out salmon flavored cat food from a can, wrinkling her nose at the smell, and changed the water bowl. "Me? Oh, well, not much. I've only been trying to figure out who murdered a sous chef and an angry baker." She frowned. "Just another day in Bijoux, apparently."

Gris let out a loud howl.

"I concur. This madness has got to stop around here. I mean, I thought I was basically returning to Mayberry, you know? I get here and suddenly people are dropping like flies." She leaned against the counter. "Huh. Maybe I *am* the link," she said, then shook her head. "Nope. It's Caleb Joseph. Everything he touches turns to murder."

A knock sounded at the front door and Morgan opened it. Cal stood there, his hair mussed from his work out, holding a bottle of wine and a bag of carry-out Italian food. *This* she could get used to.

"Who were you talking to? And did I hear my name?" he asked as he walked in and placed the items on the counter.

"Just catching up with Gris. That smells amazing."

"Gino's is the best around," Cal said with a smile. He emptied the bags and twisted the cap off the red table wine. "If you grab some glasses and plates, I'll dish this up and we can get to work."

Morgan and Cal carried their plates of lasagna, cheesy garlic bread, and glasses of wine into her spare bedroom. "This is it," she said. She placed her plate and glass on the nightstand and sat cross-legged on the floor.

Cal stood for a moment and surveyed the room. "And you've already been through all of these boxes?"

"Multiple times." She sighed and took a bite of lasagna. "Oh my god, you weren't kidding. This is amazing."

Cal sat on the wood floor, balancing his plate and glass as he did so. He found a spot, out of the way of being accidentally tipped over, and put his wine there. Forking up a full bite he groaned. "I've been looking forward to this all day."

"Going through a stack of old boxes, looking for the proverbial needle?" Morgan took a bite of the garlic bread and washed it down with a sip of wine.

He grinned. "No, the food," he said, holding up another forkful of the lasagna smothered red sauce, ricotta cheese, and mozzarella. "This too, though. I'm honored to help. I can only begin to imagine what you've gone through these past years."

"People will tell you the first few months someone is gone are the hardest. Then they say it's the first year. After that, you get told to get over it, move on. Your grief is questioned when it's held for longer than others are comfortable with."

Cal nodded. "We're not a society comfortable with death. Other cultures do it much better than we do. Some see death personified and invite it into their homes when a loved one passes. They ask Death to grieve with them."

"That's really beautiful."

"It is. And, for the record, no one should ever tell you how to mourn. We all have our own timetable for processing." He looked at Morgan. "You should have never been shamed for your grief."

Morgan's eyes met his and she thought she saw a hint of tears behind his glasses. Overwhelmed, she looked away, took another bite of food, but didn't really taste it this time. "Have you been married? I realize I don't know."

"I was, for about ten years. Her name's Diana." He sighed and brushed his dark hair away from his forehead, adjusted his glasses. "We met in college, were engaged by the time we started our master's degrees, married a year later. We were both academics, so our lives were in step with university life."

"What happened?"

"Like you, Captain Morgan, it's not something I enjoy talking about." He took another bite of food and a sip of wine, shook his head. "Suffice to say she lost her trust in us and left me the same time I resigned from my professorship. We divorced soon after. Four years ago."

"That's when you came to Bijoux?"

Cal nodded. "Uncle Baptiste had left me the Raven's Nest the year prior and I hadn't done anything with it. I always loved it here, so Bijoux seemed like a good place to start over."

"That's a theme you and I share," Morgan said with a small smile. "And I am sorry for your loss."

"Thank you. It was a long time ago and I've let most of it go. Though, as we both know, grief can come in waves and when you least expect it. You're planning a life with someone one day and the next they're gone." He shrugged, shook his head as if to clear it, looked around the room. "Anyway. What say you we get started on these boxes? They're certainly not going to sort themselves."

Morgan pushed down the sadness that crept in as she looked over at the pile of boxes and forced a smile. "Boxes will be the death of me, I swear." She stood and looked through the stacks. She'd already gone through the first five again and looked for the sixth. "Here. Box number six. You take this one and I'll take number seven. Between us, we may just get through these tonight."

Cal pulled the lid off. "Do you have an inkling of what you're looking for?"

"Specifically, any evidence Ian may have gathered against his partner, James Wheat, regarding possible links to drug deals, robberies, even murder." She sat back down and started going through her box. "Having said that, I have no idea what it could look like. Maybe a random CD or flash drive? A file folder intentionally mislabeled. Ian was always stealthy when it came to things like this, though, and would hide information in places you'd never think to look. He lived with 'just in case' in the back of his brain."

"And he never talked to you about his suspicions regarding James?"

Morgan leaned back against the bed. "That's the weird part. He never did. And we talked about everything." Morgan laughed. "Even things I'd rather not have known."

Cal was silent and Morgan looked up from the file she was thumbing through. "What?" she asked.

"He knew this investigation was going to be dangerous. He wanted to protect you."

Morgan nodded. "I think that's where his head may have been. Having said that, maybe he'd still be alive if he *had* trusted me."

"It wasn't lack of trust. You just told me you and Ian shared everything. So ask yourself, why did Ian not tell you about investigating his partner? I'd say he wanted to protect you and thought it best to keep you out of the loop until the worst was over. If I were looking at this through the lens of Detective Philip, that's what he would conclude."

"Detective Philip." Morgan snorted, not wanting to examine the truth of Cal's insight. It was too connected to her own guilty conscience. She thought she'd known Ian inside and out. *So why wasn't I able to tell that something was going on?* If she had, she might have been able to save him. "We need to get you a life," she grumbled.

Cal's gaze met hers. "I'm quite happy with the one I'm building here, thank you very much."

Morgan nodded as she busied herself with unpacking up the box. "I'm finally starting to feel more settled in Bijoux, especially since I've started the cottage rehab. It helps my brain to put things in order."

Griselda slinked into the spare room and pawed at a box lid. Before Morgan could stop the cat, she'd jumped into the box Morgan was going through and immediately curled up into a ball. "Cats and boxes, am I right?"

Cal laughed, reached into the box and scratched Gris behind her ears. Her purr shook the box. "One of the things I like about cats is they're honest. If they don't like you, you know it. And when they do, well, friends for life."

"How come you haven't gotten a cat yet? I mean, you do have those amazing pajamas your mom got you." Morgan grinned. She'd gotten a firsthand look at the PJs when she'd had to share a room with Caleb at the Firefly during the romance writers' conference a few months back.

"Actually, one of the ferals in Frankie's alley behind the Perch Mouth just had kittens. Frankie's keeping an eye on them and I'll take one or two when they're old enough to leave their mother." He grinned. "Maybe three. A bookstore should have several cats. Not only to keep the mice away, but to greet—or ignore—visitors." Cal held up a CD case. "There's an extra disc in here, between the wrapper folds. Have you looked at this?" He stretched out and handed her the disc.

Morgan turned it over. No writing on it, or any other indication it may have been used. "I haven't seen that one before. I'll grab my laptop."

When she returned a few minutes later, Morgan dropped the CD into the drive and closed the door. She realized she was holding her breath while she waited for the disc to boot and she exhaled.

"This could be it," Cal said from over her shoulder.

Morgan's hand shook as she clicked on the Folders icon and the disc file directory jumped on the screen. "Damn."

"Radiohead, Collective Soul, Montell Jordan, Blues Traveler. Nineties music?"

Morgan wiped at her eyes with the heel of her hand. "Yeah, it was his thing."

"Let's play them."

"What? No. I—I don't think I can."

Cal moved back to where he'd been sitting. "How about just one? In honor of Ian's interesting taste in music while we search for whatever evidence he left behind."

Morgan laughed. "These aren't the worse, let me tell you. He used to try to play eighties heavy metal on road trips. I just couldn't with that." She scanned the list. "Here's one he and I both loved." She adjusted the volume, hit 'play,' and smiled.

"Hard to go wrong with Tom Petty," Cal said as *You Don't Know How It Feels* filled the room. He grinned. "All right. Let's get through these."

"WELL, that's the last of them," Morgan said as she replaced the lid on the box in front of her. She checked her watch. Midnight. "Six hours later and we found nothing."

"You're not counting that nineties mix CD. Or Ian's collection of vintage keys and original Star Trek bobbleheads. There's some serious cool in there."

Morgan laughed a little. It felt good to talk about her late husband and not feel the pain and angst that usually went along with the conversations. "He definitely had his 'things.'" She grew serious. "But zero evidence. I don't know that I should be surprised. Ian was pretty good at hiding things. One time, he set up a scavenger hunt for me to find my Christmas present. Now that was annoying—" She blew out a breath and ran her fingers through her hair. "I'm realizing just how much I've focused on his death and not on his life."

"You went through a traumatic experience; it makes sense that's where your head would be. Have you thought about asking Zoe? She may be able to pick up on the energies."

"Energies? Who are you? And no. I'm not going down that road."

"Why are you so set against using the tools available to you?"

"Wow, you just called my stepmom a tool. You won't be getting any more coffee cake."

Cal held firm. "You know what I meant."

"Look, some detectives like the idea of using so-called psychics to help their investigations. For myself, I've never bought into the idea." She wadded up a napkin and threw it at him. "Come on. I think you'd know that about me by now."

Cal caught it and threw it back, laughing. "I have and you are a true skeptic. But you can't discount that she's been right several times about our cases."

"Oh, they're *our* cases now?" Morgan grinned and shook her head.

"Of course. You're my research, remember? So, are you thinking Ian may have left clues elsewhere as to where any evidence could be hidden?" Cal asked.

"Honestly, I have no idea. What I do know is I'm exhausted." She gave him a half smile. "I have to get up early and get back to work on the bake-off murders, so I'm throwing you out."

Cal pushed himself off the floor. "At least this is one of the nicer places I've been tossed out of." He gathered up their dirty dishes and carried them to the kitchen. "I feel like I know Ian much better now. I'll keep thinking about this."

Morgan gave him a quick hug and whispered, "Thank you. For everything." She stepped away. "You're a good human, Caleb Joseph."

He raised an eyebrow. "Remember that the next time you're angry with me."

CHAPTER 17

Officer down...

Pull the sheet back. Let me see him. I have to see him.

Strong arms slipped around her, settled her, whispered in her ear. You already have the answers.

Morgan shoved at her pillow and sat up. She pushed her hair out of her eyes, pulled the covers back onto the bed from where she'd kicked them off onto the floor.

You already have the answers.

"No, I don't have the answers," she said out loud, frustration running through her. "Dammit, Ian. Why did you have to make this so hard?" She punched at the air, sobbing. "I'm done! I'm done! I give! I can't do this anymore!"

Griselda jumped up on the nightstand and stared at Morgan. Morgan stared back. "I'm not in the mood for a play date."

The cat walked in several tight circles, then sat down on top of a small carved wood box.

"Come on, Gris. Don't sit on that." Morgan pried the box out from under the cat's behind. "Seriously. We need to discuss boundaries." Morgan laid back on her pillow, pulled the covers up under her arms, and turned the box over in her hands. The keepsake had been crafted out of walnut, hand-carved with an image of the tattoo she and Ian shared—a winged heart with a knife through it. Ian had commissioned it to hold her engagement ring, a gorgeous round black sapphire surrounded by diamonds set in white gold. She'd put the ring in there for safe keeping, about a year after he was gone, when she'd finally felt able to remove it.

Morgan turned on the lamp, gently opened the box, and slid the ring on. Admiring the sparkle in the lamplight, grief flowed through her. She took a deep breath, exhaled all of it, returned the ring to the box. As she started to place the box back on the nightstand, she noticed the bottom of it didn't fit as tight against one of the sides. *No, it couldn't be.* She pulled a pocketknife out of her nightstand drawer and pried at the bottom. As it popped off, a micro flash drive fell out and landed in her lap.

A sob escaped her. *I've looked at this box so many times, how did I miss this?* She picked up the drive. *Because I wasn't looking beyond Ian's things.* Of course, he would have hidden this where no one would ever think to look. "I love you," she whispered. She threw the covers back and ran to grab her laptop.

Sitting at the kitchen counter, she plugged the drive in, and opened the folder. Morgan caught her breath. Here was everything Ian had gathered against James. Files with off shore bank account information showing large deposits. Surveillance photos. A log of James's activities and meetings with known drug dealers. She grabbed her phone and called Liz.

"Morgan? It's 3 a.m. Are you okay?"

"I found it."

"Wait. What?"

"Ian's files on James. I found them. I'll upload everything to the cloud and send you the link."

"No. Don't email anything. I'm still not sure there isn't a leak at the station. I'll come there."

"I can bring it to you. You don't need to make the trip."

"Absolutely not. One, I don't want you near Detroit when this breaks. There could be repercussions and threats from James's cronies. Two, you're in the middle of a murder investigation. No. I'll head there tomorrow."

"Okay. I'm having a remembrance fire in the evening, after the bake-off ends. It's the sixth anniversary. Join me on the beach in front of the cottage, then we'll go through the files."

"Sounds like a perfect way to celebrate Ian *and* finding the evidence. Try to get some rest. I love you. I'll see you soon."

"Love you, too, friend," Morgan said and disconnected the call. She removed the thumb drive from the laptop, placed it back in the bottom of the ring box, and popped the thin piece of wood back in place. Instead of returning it to the nightstand, she went to her closet and put it in her gun safe. "No sense in taking any chances with this," she said to Gris, who had moved to the center of the bed. Morgan picked up the large cat, gave her a gentle squeeze, and curled back up under the covers with the feline. "You're my hero."

CHAPTER 18

"Hey, good morning," Morgan said as she entered the station. "What did you find on Bobby and Eva? Are they dirty?"

"Nope, squeaky clean," JJ said. He handed Morgan the background checks on the eliminated bakers.

"Tell me about Benny's laptop." Morgan dropped the reports on her desk and dragged her desk chair over next to JJ's. She'd been on her way to the community center when JJ had called her about the data recovery.

JJ tapped on his keyboard and started reading aloud:

"Greetings, fans, from the Baker's Dozen Hometown Cupcake Bake-Off in Bijoux, Michigan. As you know from my last post, I was booted unceremoniously from the show. I stand by my accusations that Queen Sass and/or her minion, Damon, tampered with my bakes. The "Queen" has had it in for me ever since I ended our romance. But that's all old news. You want the new dish, don't you? What I'm about to say will blow the lid off Sassy McComas's empire and bring it tumbling down."

Morgan rolled her eyes. "Drama, much?"

"No kidding," JJ said, and continued:

"I have it on good authority cheating is afoot with the cupcake bakers this season. And that Sassy herself knows all about it. There's even been speculation the departed Pierre Brahman was in on the subterfuge and encouraged "the cheating baker" to falsify their recipes in order to get ahead and create show drama. Which, as we know, really brings in the viewers. Of course, the implications of this will ultimately ruin the Baker's Dozen reputation, along with Sassy's and the new show she has in the works. I mean, if you can't trust the queen, who can you trust? Hahahahaha. Scoot your chairs closer, kiddies, and I'll reveal who the cheat is."

JJ stopped reading and sat back in his chair.

"Is that it? Did he name the baker?"

"Not that I can find. The post stops there. It's possible the last part of the file was too corrupted to restore."

"Or he was killed before he could write it. Which means the killer knew Benny was onto something. And he wasn't wrong, Sassy would have a lot to lose if word got out her show was encouraging cheating." Morgan checked her phone. "The bake-off finale starts in an hour. Let's you and I go have a chat with Queen Sass."

Morgan pulled the department's blue Ford Ranger up along the curb in front of Hannah's Heavenly Confections. Zoe was behind the counter, boxing up a variety of baked treats for a customer. Next door, Wendy Peltier was arranging hanks of what appeared to be hand dyed yarn in the front window. Morgan exited the truck and Wendy waved and stepped out of her shop.

"Good morning, Morgan," Wendy said with a smile. She nodded toward Hannah's. "Here for a sweet breakfast? I'm likely to gain twenty pounds just from the amazing aromas."

Morgan laughed. "I completely understand. How's the set-up going? Were you able to get past your brother's beautification edict?"

"So far. I decided to officially join the ranks of the Hold-Outs. We even had a meeting last night to figure out how to fight Ed." She rolled her eyes. "He's always been bossy, even when we were kids."

"The Hold-Outs are organizing? That sounds like something Cal would instigate. He owns the Raven's Nest."

"Oh, yes. He is one of the business owner's leading the charge. He wasn't there last night, but I hear he's even floating the idea of running for mayor."

"How do you feel about that?"

Wendy shrugged. "I think it's a good idea. Ed needs to expand his life beyond terrorizing business owners. The old has to be allowed to exist alongside the new, otherwise we forget the past and it also becomes more challenging to go forward. We need balance, don't you think?"

Morgan nodded. She couldn't disagree, it was exactly how she'd been feeling lately about her own life.

"That Cal, though. I've met him. He's yummy." Wendy laughed. "My mom would've called him a tall, cool drink of water."

Yummy? Morgan felt her stomach catch. *You're just hungry. But what kind of hungry?* her inner voice answered itself. *Nope, not that kind.* "Good luck fighting the good fight. I hear a muffin and latte calling my name." Morgan grinned and walked into Hannah's.

Zoe was ringing out the customer who was thanking her for saving his hide as it was his wife's birthday and he'd forgotten until that morning. "Hopefully these treats and a dozen roses will do the trick," he said to Zoe.

Morgan recognized the person in line as Dr. Robert Dudley, one of Bijoux's two local dentists, the other being his wife, Dr. Roberta Dudley. *What are the chances of two dentists with essentially the same name ending up together?*

"I'm sure Roberta is going to love both." Zoe smiled. "Wish her happy birthday from me."

The phone began to ring just as Zoe was handing Dr. Dudley his change. "Hi, Morgan," Zoe called out on her way to answer it. "I'll be with you in a moment."

Morgan exchanged pleasantries with Dr. Dudley and also wished his wife a happy birthday.

"Weren't you supposed to come in for a check-up with Roberta?" Dr. Dudley asked Morgan.

"Yes, sorry, I had to cancel at the last minute—but I'll definitely reschedule."

"Good, I'll let Roberta know. Take care, now." Dr. Dudley smiled and left.

"That was the third birthday cake order this morning on the phone," Zoe said grabbing a cloth to wipe down the counter. "Luckily, Hannah won't have to fill them until next weekend. Now, my dear, what will you have this fine morning? Wait, let me guess. A breakfast muffin and a chai latte."

"*You* are a good guesser. That will be perfect," Morgan said. She leaned on the glass case. "Do you recall selling cupcakes to any of the bake-off bakers this past week?"

Zoe slid the cup of milk into the frothing machine. "Of course," she said over her shoulder. "Most of the bakers have been in here. I assumed they were either tired of their own baking or checking out the competition."

"Maybe a little of both." Morgan glanced around. *Good, they were alone.* "As you know, Hannah's cupcakes were found at both of the murder scenes. I'm trying to pinpoint who might have had access to them."

Zoe placed the latte and a chocolate chip and oat breakfast muffin in front of Morgan. Morgan raised an eyebrow. "Oats?"

Zoe grinned. "Fiber. It'll help your mood. As far as customers go, it could be any number of people, including the bakers. Like I said, near as I can tell, they've all been in here. Oh, that tall British guy from the show, too. What's his name? He was here."

"Damon?"

"Yes! Damon. And not Sassy—the other woman, Bean."

"Did they come in together?"

Zoe thought for a moment. "No, different times. If I recall correctly, Bean was here Thursday evening. I remember that because it was right before closing time and Hannah was showing me the ropes around here. A dozen vanilla cupcakes, I think."

"That would be an unfortunate coincidence," Cal said, closing the shop door behind him. "Pierre had a vanilla cupcake in his hand, didn't he?"

"Why are you here?"

"Why does anyone stop off at a bake shop?" he asked, eyes narrowed. "Stop being so suspicious."

"It's my job to be suspicious."

"I can attest to that," Frankie said, entering the shop behind Cal. "I saw you both in here, thought I'd stop in." She smiled. "Even when we were kids, Morgan had a suspicious nature. I remember a speech she wrote called, *That Super Sneaky Santa Claus,* in third grade."

"Is this 'gang up' on Morgan day?" Morgan asked. "Because—and

I'm so sorry—but I didn't have it on my calendar so it's going to have to wait."

Zoe laughed and packed up a cheese croissant stuffed with bacon and eggs for Frankie and steel-cut oatmeal with flax seed and goji berries for Cal.

Morgan covered a smile. *No doubt, he's doing penance after last night's lasagna.*

Cal held his bag up. "Before you ask, I called ahead."

"Me too," Frankie added.

As Cal and Frankie turned to leave, Morgan said, "Hey, Cal, thank you again for your help last night." She looked at Frankie. "Liz will be here later tonight, FYI."

Frankie smiled. "Yeah, she texted. Okay if I join you two?"

"What's going on this evening?" Cal asked. "And, more importantly, why wasn't I invited?"

"I'm having what I'm calling a Letting Go fire on the beach tonight. It's six years today since Ian died. I'm sending him off." She glanced away. "It was only going to be me and Gris, but after last night, Liz will be here. Frankie too, now." She smiled at the other woman. "And yes, you're welcome to join, Cal. Especially after last night." She looked over at Zoe.

"Thank you but no. Four is the perfect number but do let your dad and me know if we can help with anything."

"I'll see you later then," Cal said. "Need to get these over to Henry."

As Cal left, Frankie focused on Morgan. "What is going on here?"

"What are you talking about?"

"That whole—*Oh, darling, I appreciate you so much can I run my hands through your hair now*—vibe with Cal." Frankie hugged her arms around herself and made kissing noises.

Morgan burst out laughing and Zoe giggled from behind the counter. "There is a definite vibration between the two of you," Zoe said. "Would you like me to look into it for you?"

"As in do a reading? No. No thank you." She stuck her tongue out at Frankie. "And there's nothing going on. He just came over last night and helped me go through the rest of Ian's things, trying to find evidence."

"Did you find any?" Frankie asked.

"I did, actually. It's why Liz is heading to town, to pick it up directly from me."

Frankie hugged her friend. "Oh, Morgan, that's wonderful news." Frankie's phone pinged. "I gotta go, but I want the whole scoop tonight."

"You got it." Morgan looked at Zoe, who was smiling. "What?"

"I'm happy for you, that's all. It seems your life is finally moving. Movement is good."

"Maybe," Morgan said. "I'm still feeling my way through it." She gathered up her muffin and latte. "Off to hunt the bad guys. Please let me know if you think of anything else regarding visits from anyone associated with the show."

"Will do. And Morgan?"

Morgan paused with the door half open.

"Do be careful."

"Is that a premonition?"

"Just common sense. There's a lot going on." Zoe smiled. "Both JJ and Cal have your back, though. Let them."

CHAPTER 19

MORGAN SWUNG by the station and picked up JJ on her way to the community center.

"I ran as many searches as I could without a warrant, "JJ said. "I've reached out to Ed, but haven't heard back yet. I did email him the paperwork, so he only needs to sign and get it back to me."

"Did you find anything significant?"

"You know, I can only go so deep. But I did discover baker Paul is a tech millionaire, so he doesn't need the money."

"A tech millionaire? Are you kidding me? Why is he on a cooking show?"

JJ rolled his shoulders and neck. "Who knows. He's probably a huge nerd when you get to know him and he thinks baking helps with the ladies."

"You do know nerds are cool, right? That at least tells us money isn't a driving factor for him. If he's that wealthy, then maybe he's driven to succeed and saw Pierre and Benny in the way of that." Morgan pulled into the parking lot and angled into a spot. "Anything else?"

"I found a couple of 'Fund My Cause' accounts online—one under Meg's name and one for Eva."

"Sounds like they needed money for something. People often set those accounts up to pay large, unexpected bills."

"Sometimes they're used to benefit community projects, too. They're not always for personal situations. I should be able to find out more once the mayor signs off on the warrants."

Morgan turned off the truck and turned slightly in her seat. "What do you think the link is between Pierre and Benny's deaths? What's your theory?"

"Just looking at what we know so far, obviously both were part of the same baking show. Benny was concerned about cheating. We have no idea what Pierre wanted to talk to Bean about. Could it have been the same subject? Sure. As far as theories go?" He rubbed his forehead. "Let's say Pierre and Benny knew who the cheater was—assuming that's what's going on—and that person took them both out to protect their identity."

"Okay. Let's say for the moment cheating was Pierre's concern as well. Who has the most benefit to gain? Obviously, the bakers. Ten thousand dollars is a lot. But the even bigger prize of a hundred thousand is more believable for motive. And a potential spot on Sassy's new show," Morgan said.

"I can believe someone would kill for a hundred thousand more than ten thousand though, of course, people have been murdered for a lot less money," JJ added.

They exited the truck and headed into the community center. "Let's focus on the remaining bakers and anyone else who's been vocal about getting eliminated, here or on social media," Morgan said.

"Captain—," JJ began.

Morgan held up a hand. "We'll start with Paul and Meg. Add Eva into the mix based on your research. Look JJ, I don't like it either, but we have to look into Hannah as well. Are you aware of any large debt she might be carrying?"

JJ grumbled, "Just the bakery. She took out a loan for new equipment last year when she opened. While she does good business, some months can be tight." He stopped walking and threw up his hands. "Look, we both know Hannah is incapable of murder."

Morgan didn't answer and kept walking. She had to maintain her objectivity, as much as she was struggling to do so. She reached the door to the gym first and held it open, waiting for JJ to catch up. "We follow the evidence."

"BAKERS, WE ASSEMBLE IN THIRTY MINUTES," Damon called out.

Paul and Hannah looked at each other, smiled, and headed toward the cafeteria. Meg must already be there, Morgan mused, as she didn't see the other woman. And where was Sassy? She scanned the gym. The host must be in her makeshift office in the classroom down the hall.

"Good morning, Captain, Deputy," Damon said as he approached Morgan and JJ. "What can I do for you today? Our schedule is quite intense with it being the last day, you know. Not a lot of free time for unscheduled interruptions."

"I'm looking for Sassy."

Damon sighed deeply. "Is it possible, at all, to wait until we finish today? The Queen is under a great deal of pressure, as are we all."

Morgan looked at him more closely. His clothes were rumpled and the thick eyeliner he wore couldn't disguise the fatigue in his eyes. "Not sleeping?" she asked.

"Not as well as I'd like, if you must know. As I said, there's a lot of pressure on everyone this weekend."

"So you're not worried that your sous chef and one of your bakers are dead? That's not what's keeping you up?"

Damon straightened. "I'd assume that goes without saying."

"How do you think something like two deaths would affect the show's ratings?" Morgan asked.

"I honestly haven't thought that far ahead," Damon answered.

"I'd think it could go either way," JJ replied. "Benny had a big following. People would likely tune in to see his final appearance."

"Is there something you both need?" Sassy asked as she approached the trio. "We're awfully busy today, you know."

Morgan turned to the older woman. "So we've been told. What can you tell me about allegations of cheating this weekend?"

Sassy's hand flew to her throat and Damon stepped close to her side. "I have no idea what you're talking about," Sassy replied.

"That was quite a reaction for not having any knowledge of such a thing," JJ said. "It seems there's something you're not telling us."

Sassy looked around. "Fine. There was a rumor, but there's *always* a rumor, I tell you. Nothing of which I have proof."

Bean entered the conversation. "I'm almost certain that's what Pierre wanted to talk to me about."

"What makes you say that?" Morgan asked.

"Just a feeling. And he may have mentioned the 'c' word." Bean wrung her hands together. "I am sorry I didn't tell you that yesterday. I didn't want to tarnish the show."

"Oh, please," Sassy said. "You'd do whatever you could to end me."

Bean straightened. "I believe it's always worked in the reverse, *you* always accusing *me* of horrible things. Maybe that's why Pierre was going to come to me, rather than you. He knew you'd be defensive whereas I would have listened to him."

Sassy scoffed. "You only listened because he bedded you."

"And a fine bedder he was! But that's neither here nor there, is it?" Bean shifted her focus to Morgan and JJ. "The bakers have to bring their own, original recipes to the competition. You might already know this, but Pierre reviews them. If he believed a recipe had been copied from another baker, he would have reported it." She bowed her head. "Or at least tried to."

"Yes, Hannah told me he looked everything over for originality and quality," Morgan said.

Sassy nodded. "That is correct. I can't imagine something like this would be the death of him, though. It's only ten thousand dollars."

"But there is the ultimate prize of a hundred thousand, isn't there?" JJ asked.

"However, if money is the motivating factor, you'd have to assume whoever killed Pierre would be assured of winning somehow. And the only way to guarantee something like that would perhaps be to have an 'in' with the staff," Morgan observed.

They all looked at Sassy. She held her hands up. "Absolutely not. I will not stand here and be accused of cheating on my own television show." She stomped her foot. "I simply will not have it."

Damon patted her back and she leaned against him. "There, there, Queen. No need to get those feathers ruffled right before we start shooting today." He stared hard at Morgan and JJ. "This interrogation is over."

"I wonder, though," Bean started, "if Pierre's death has anything to do with Benny Staples's suicide? They hardly seem connected, other than to the show. But I do wonder." She smiled. "I watch quite a bit of *Sherlock Holmes*. Who, by the way, would have solved the case by now and would be enjoying a nice sit by the fire with a beverage at this point."

Morgan shrugged off the Holmes comparison. *Good. They still think Benny killed himself.* "We have some evidence suggesting a possible connection, but nothing I'm able to discuss at the moment," Morgan said. "If you don't mind, JJ and I would like to hang around for a bit and observe the bakers."

"Do we have a choice?" Sassy sneered.

"No, not really," Morgan said. "I appreciate you have a show to produce, but the investigation has to come first." Morgan's phone rang. "Excuse me, I need to take this. JJ, I'll meet you in there."

Morgan stepped outside and took the call. "Good morning."

"Did you get any sleep last night?" Liz asked.

"Some. It's the last day of the baking show. JJ and I are here talking to people, looking around." Morgan looked up, breathed. The sky was cloudless and held the promise of good weather for her plans this evening.

"I just wanted to let you know I'll be leaving here in a couple of hours. I need to get the dog sitter lined up for Beef."

Beef was Liz's gray pit bull, a sweetheart of a dog with humans, but not a lover of cats. "Sounds good. I'll see you this evening."

"Oh, and if the implication wasn't clear, you *will* have an overnight guest," Liz said, laughing.

"Yeah, I got that. And thanks for being there Liz."

CHAPTER 20

THE MORNING BAKE-OFF challenge of savory flavors triggered angst and worry among the remaining competitors, but that was it as far as drama went. Now it was time for each of the final three bakers to present their wares. "Hannah is going to do great," Morgan whispered to JJ.

"I hope so. I'll be happy when this show is over and things can get back to normal." He glanced at Morgan. "And we've solved the case, of course."

"Paul, would you please bring your savory cupcakes to the judging table and tell us about them?" Damon instructed.

Paul walked up to the dais and placed his display of twenty-four cupcakes in a wood crate lined with green checkered cloth on the table. He stepped back. "This morning, I've created a smoked ghost pepper and anejo cheesecake with a tequila reduction glaze drizzled over the top. It's reminiscent of my time spent in Mexico."

Bean took a bite and immediately started fanning her mouth. She grabbed a glass of water and took several sips. "Did you leave the seeds in the pepper?" she asked.

Sassy and Bean each inspected the sponge.

"I did." He frowned. "Too spicy? I'm so sorry."

Sassy waved her hand and took a bite. "My palate isn't as heat sensitive as my fellow judge. I think the amount of pepper to cheese is almost there but a bit less heat would be better. I would have removed the seeds. Besides the spice, they give an unseemly crunch, which I quite do not enjoy."

Paul carried his crate back to his station, his head bowed.

"Meg? Please come forward," Damon said.

Meg approached cautiously, biting her bottom lip, and placed her large ceramic platter lined with a floral fabric on the table. "I've gone Italian this morning. My cupcakes are filled with pesto and I used ricotta cheese in my buttercream icing. Topped with roasted pine nuts, as you can see."

"Interesting," Sassy said. "And reminiscent of something I can't put my finger on."

"A plate of pesto, perhaps?" Bean asked with a sly smile.

Sassy frowned. "Perhaps. The sponge is a bit dry. Having said that, you've used too much olive oil in your pesto. It's soaked the bottom." She wagged her finger at Meg. "And if there's one thing we do not like, it's soggy bottoms."

"I'm enjoying the ricotta buttercream, though," Bean added. "Decent job with that, though I think it needs to be a bit sweeter to counteract the sourness of the cheese."

Meg slumped and removed her tray.

"That leaves Hannah. Would you please step forward?"

Hannah walked to the front, her head high, carrying a wire basket lined with turquoise fabric, and filled with her cupcakes. "Today, I've made breakfast cupcakes. A vanilla sponge with bacon in the mix, maple flavored swiss meringue, with a brown sugar bacon topping."

"Well, you certainly can't go wrong with bacon now, can you?" Sassy said. She picked up a cupcake and sniffed it. "Smells lovely. Let's see how it tastes."

"Oh, my. That bacon and maple meringue really is special," Sassy said.

"You've outdone yourself with this combination, Hannah dear," Bean added. "One of the best bites this entire weekend."

"Wow," Hannah said. "Thank you both so much!" She carried her basket back to her station and smiled over at JJ and Morgan.

"And cut!" the director shouted. The crew broke down their gear and stacked it off to the side, before exiting the gym.

Damon stepped forward. "Now, bakers, we'll take a two hour break before the final bake this afternoon. Please clean up your stations. As you know, lunch is available in the cafeteria."

Damon, Sassy, and Bean left the gym as the bakers began wiping down their work areas down. JJ and Morgan stood across the counter from Hannah. "That was excellent!" he said.

"Maybe. You're only as good as your last bake, though," Hannah said.

Morgan glanced at the other two bakers, who weren't looking nearly as happy as Hannah. Paul, in particular, was frowning as he finished organizing his supplies. His eyes met Morgan's and he immediately looked away. *Okay then.*

"That was some harsh criticism for you two," Morgan said. "Especially considering how well you've both been doing."

"We all have off bakes. It's the nature of the beast," Paul said. "You have to stay focused on the next one, or you lose your mojo."

"I'm used to being criticized so, you know, whatever," Meg said with a shrug. She folded her apron neatly and placed it on her counter. "I'm going to get some food."

At the mention of food, Morgan's stomach growled. She checked the time. Twelve-fifteen. The show would reconvene at two. "JJ, I'm going to head over to Dave's for some lunch. You want to come along?"

"Or I could have lunch here, with Hannah," he said, looking at his girlfriend.

Hannah glanced away. "I need to focus on what I'm doing this afternoon. We'll talk when the show is over, okay?"

"Um, yeah. Sure. I'll see you later," he said quietly and walked toward the exit.

"Hey, kids, what'll you have today?" Jerome asked.

"Cheeseburger and fries, please. And iced tea," Morgan said.

"JJ? How about you?"

"I'm not really hungry." He sighed. "I guess I'll have the Truck Stop breakfast with scrambled eggs and a chocolate milkshake."

"That's a lot of food for someone who's not hungry," Cal observed as he slid into the booth next to Morgan.

"Have you stuck a tracking device on me? Is that how you always manage to know where I am?"

"Saw your truck out front." Cal laughed, then grew serious. "However, I do like that idea."

"No. You are not going to track me."

"I mean for Detective Philip so he can track the perp. That's cop talk for perpetrator."

"We know what perp means, for heaven's sake. Who do you think you're talking to?"

"So, what's up with our boy here?" Cal gestured at JJ, who was staring solemnly out the window.

"Hannah trouble."

"Ah. There's nothing like a problem with a woman to put a man in a mood."

"What century are you from? Do you realize how sexist that sounds?"

"It's not sexist when it works both ways. I've seen more than one woman in a mood over a man."

Morgan snorted and shoved playfully at his arm. "Likely from you." That made JJ laugh.

"There he is," Cal said with a smile. "Hey, how can I help?"

Jerome placed Morgan and JJ's beverages on the table and took Cal's order of Cobb Salad with dressing on the side and a lemonade.

"Appreciate it, buddy. Hannah is not happy with me and I'm still figuring out a way around that."

"You can't go 'around' things, JJ. You have to deal with them head on and talk it out," Morgan said.

"I would, but she won't. You heard her earlier." He rolled his eyes. "We'll talk after the show." He rubbed his midsection. "My stomach doesn't feel so good."

Cal reached across the table and patted JJ's shoulder. "And that is the price of love, my friend." He drew his arm back and sipped the lemonade Jerome had just set in front of him. "I know Hannah cares for you—loves you. And I know you feel the same for her. I believe love always wins, so I'm certain the two of you will work it out."

Morgan's jaw dropped and she snapped it closed, stared at Cal. "That was an incredibly sweet thing to say."

"You forget, Captain." He adjusted his glasses and looked at her. "I am a romance writer. Being a hopeful romantic is part of the job description." He considered JJ. "Plus, I know our guy here. He's a good man. I trust he'll figure it out."

JJ offered a wan smile. "Thanks, man."

"So, what's next on our agenda today?"

"*Our*?" Morgan asked. "Why do I have to keep reminding you there's no 'we' or 'our' when it comes to police work?"

"What can I say? I'm stubborn. Plus research for my breakout detective novel."

Morgan shook her head, popped a fry in her mouth, and mulled over what she was going to do with Caleb Joseph. "Since it seems we're going to be forever stuck with you, you're going to have to sign a waiver releasing the Bijoux Police of any liability should something happen to you while you're with us."

"What? That's ridiculous. Of course I wouldn't hold any of you responsible if something happened to me."

"You might not, but what about your family? If you were, say, killed while we're working a case, they'd have every right to sue for damages."

"That won't happen."

"And you tagging along from now on won't happen without signing the document." Morgan watched his body language. Cal crossed his arms, stared at her, looked at JJ who was back to looking out the window.

"You don't trust me."

"That's a reach, Cal. You know I trust you or I wouldn't have allowed you to help me last night. This is about business."

"The captain is good at separating facts from feelings," JJ said. "She still thinks Hannah could've killed Pierre and Benny."

Cal's eyes widened. "You don't."

Morgan shook her head at JJ, but didn't answer.

"You do." Cal leaned back in the booth and whistled. "Well, we can't be surprised by this, JJ. You know Morgan's credo when it comes to cases."

"That I do. She's reminded me often lately."

"You both know we can't assume someone is innocent just because they're a friend. Or girlfriend. We have to follow the evidence." She pushed her plate of food away, no longer hungry. "Honestly, I don't like it any better than either of you do." Morgan checked her phone. "It's 1:30. Let's head back to the center. Assuming the murderer is connected with the show, we only have today left to find them."

CHAPTER 21

IT WAS ONE-FORTY-FIVE WHEN MORGAN, JJ, and Cal entered the gym. The camera crew was assembled, lights positioned at opposite sides of each workstation, and everything was spruced up and ready for the final bake-off taping.

"I see you're back," Damon said as he approached the trio. He'd changed into a dark floral overshirt with a *Blondie* t-shirt underneath. He looked at Cal. "Did you need more books?"

"No, I'm with them. I'm consulting for the Bijoux Police now."

"Wait a minute," Morgan said.

"As soon as we finalize the paperwork," Cal added. "For the moment, I'm a silent observer."

"Yeah, no one could ever accuse you of being silent," JJ said.

Cal squinted at JJ. "I can be quite silent, and stealthy, when required. It's part of my training, you now."

Not again with the training, Morgan thought. "Can we please move along? Damon, do you know where the bakers are?"

"Actually, they should be in here at this point, readying themselves for the finals. They're likely in the cafeteria and lost track of time. If you'll excuse me, I need to go get them." Damon walked through the doors to the cafeteria, then immediately turned back around. "They're not in there. They know how important this final shoot is." He glanced around the gym. "Where could they have gone off to?"

Morgan's senses tingled. "Is there anywhere else they might be? Another lounge, maybe?"

"No, none. If they don't show up soon, we're going to fall behind schedule. Sassy does not like it when we're late." Damon grimaced. "It is not a pretty sight."

"I'm sure it's not," Morgan said. "I'll go check the kitchen. JJ, please check the restrooms."

"What would you like me to do?" Cal asked.

"Not get yourself killed," Morgan replied.

"You're funny today," Cal said as he followed her into the cafeteria kitchen.

Morgan shrugged. "It's part of *my* charm."

Cal laughed, then stopped when Morgan held up her hand. The back door to the alley was partially open and she could hear voices. She walked quietly to the door, peeked out, then pulled back. She grabbed her phone and texted JJ. *They're in the alley. Go around from the outside but be quiet. Don't let them see you.*

"What's happening?" Cal whispered.

Morgan held a finger up to her lips and drew her gun. She gently pushed the door open with her free hand. "Hey. What's going on out here?" she asked.

Paul, Hannah, and Meg all looked at her at the same time. Paul was standing off to the side, near the back of the narrow dead end alley. Hannah was against the brick wall of the next building over and Meg was standing next to her, a butcher knife in one hand, one of Hannah's cupcakes in the other.

Meg glanced over her shoulder. "This doesn't concern either of you. This is bakers' business."

"Come on, Meg," Paul said. "Put the knife down and let's talk about this."

"Back off Paul, or I'll hurt your girlfriend here."

"She's not my girlfriend and I object to the implication. So would my actual girlfriend."

"Whatever, Paul." Meg refocused on Hannah. "Take a bite. It's one of yours so, of course, it's delicious, right?"

"Why do you want to kill me?" Hannah asked. Her eyes met Morgan's.

Morgan could see the fear running through her friend. "It seems Hannah's pretty full from her lunch," Morgan said softly. "Drop the knife and the cupcake, Meg. Let's talk about this. I don't want to hurt you."

"I'm already hurt, can't you see that?" Her hand with the knife drooped a little and Hannah suddenly stomped on Meg's instep and made a run for it, toward JJ who sprinted toward Hannah.

Meg yowled, dropped the knife, and stumbled against the brick wall. Morgan holstered her gun, grabbed her handcuffs, and snapped them on Meg before the woman knew what was happening.

JJ held Hannah by her upper arms, looked her over. "Are you okay?"

Hannah nodded, then started sobbing. JJ pulled her close. "You're safe now," he murmured.

Morgan led Meg into the cafeteria, stating Meg's legal rights as they walked, and sat her down on a bench. She straddled the one opposite Meg, and Cal stood behind her.

"What is the ruckus all about?" Sassy asked as she entered the cafeteria, Damon and Bean following after her. "We heard shouting."

"I'm just getting ready to find out," Morgan replied. She looked at Meg and asked one question. "Why?"

Meg lowered her head and tears ran down her cheeks. "You wouldn't understand."

"I promise I'll try to. Now, why did you want to kill Hannah?"

Meg's head shot up. "I wasn't trying to kill her. It was never my intention to kill anyone." She burst into tears, her hands covering her face. "I only wanted to make her sick, so she couldn't compete." She looked at Sassy. "I have to win. Please."

"Why is it so important to you?" Cal asked. "Why would you go this far to win?"

"My dad. He needs round the clock medical care. He and my mom are losing their house to the bills. I needed the money to help them."

"The Fund My Cause donation page," Morgan said.

Meg nodded. "If you saw it, then you know it didn't bring in much money. I need to win. The ten thousand dollars would be enough to save their home."

"Tell me about Pierre. If you didn't mean to kill anyone, what happened there?"

Meg lowered her head and shook it side to side. "When he saw my recipes, he recognized them. I'm not a good creative baker, never been able to come up with my own formulas." She glanced up at the hosts. "I found some really old ones of Sassy's online."

"That's why your pesto cupcake tasted familiar," Sassy said. "You pinched my recipe."

"I did and I'm so sorry. I only wanted to make Pierre sick, so he couldn't tell you." She looked pleadingly at Sassy. "Honest."

Sassy refused to meet Meg's eyes. "Please take her away, Captain. We need to finish filming and I'm sure you need to continue questioning her." Sassy turned to Hannah and Paul, who were off to the side with JJ. "You two will still compete, yes?"

Hannah looked up at Paul and took a deep breath. "Yes. Yes, I will compete."

"As will I," Paul said with a smile, his eyes on Hannah.

Morgan pulled Meg to her feet. "Are you going to stay here?" she asked JJ. "How about you, Cal?"

"Yeah, if you're okay with it. I'd like to keep an eye on things," JJ said in a tight voice, shooting a scowl at Paul.

"Henry is coming over to watch the final judging and I told him I'd meet him here," Cal replied. "Unless you need me to help with something?"

"No worries. I got this," Morgan said and led Meg to her truck.

BACK AT THE POLICE STATION, Morgan secured Meg in one of the three holding cells. She stood, arms crossed, and observed the other woman. "What about Benny?"

"What about him?" Meg asked.

"Was his death an accident as well? And then you made it look like a suicide afterward?"

Meg stood. "Wait. What? Benny killed himself. Everyone knows that. I didn't have anything to do his death."

"You're telling me you didn't kill him?" Morgan leaned in. "He was going to expose you."

Meg started pacing in the small cell. "I swear, I had no idea about any of that. I've already confessed about Pierre. I promise you, Pierre's death *was* an accident. I never intended to kill him." She sat on the edge of the cot. "I'm not good with measurements. After it happened, I figured out the dose, so I knew how to just make Hannah sick, not kill her." She wrung her hands together. "I didn't like Benny, that's not a secret. Nor was it a secret that he didn't like me. You were there the first day, and heard what he said. But I absolutely didn't kill him."

Morgan considered Meg's words. If what she said was true, then there was another killer in Bijoux. She texted JJ what Meg had said, told him to keep an eye out and be careful. She pocketed the keys to the holding cell and grabbed several bottled waters and protein bars and handed them through the bars to the other woman. "Someone will be by in a few hours with dinner, but this should hold you until then. Tomorrow, you'll be moved to Odawa County jail to await your hearing and trial. An attorney will be assigned to you when you arrive, unless you already have one."

"No, I don't have an attorney. I've never needed one. I have to call my mom, let her know."

Morgan nodded and handed Meg the station phone. When she'd disconnected the call, a teary-eyed Meg said, "T-thank you. And I really am sorry."

CHAPTER 22

MORGAN DROVE DOWN MAIN STREET, toward the community center and the bake-off finals. Her dad and Zoe were out in front of the hardware store, setting up an array of snow shovels. She pulled the truck alongside the curb. "Isn't it a little early in the season for those?" she asked with a laugh. "It is only September, you know."

"You haven't been here through the winter for a while," Able said. "Snow can happen when you least expect it." He eyed the shovels then grabbed one of the medium-sized lighter ones and put it in the back of the truck. "Don't say I never gave you anything," he said with a wink.

"You want to come in for a cuppa?" Zoe asked.

"Normally, yes. But I need to get over to the center. We solved Pierre's case today, but Benny's is still outstanding."

"You've made an arrest?" Able asked. He leaned his arm on the truck. "Who is it? Motive?"

"Always the cop," Morgan said with a smile. "It was Meg. Her parents apparently have enormous medical bills and are losing their home. She says killing Pierre was an accident."

"You believe her?"

"I do, actually. She also says she had nothing to do with Benny's death."

"Well, that's a twist," Zoe said. "I've started reading the new cozy mystery series by Joann Angel. It's terrific," she explained. "They call something like this a 'plot twist' when it happens."

"A twist for sure," Morgan said.

"Morgan? Be careful," Zoe added.

"Always. I'll talk to you later," she said. Able patted the truck and stepped away. Morgan waved and drove off.

"How's Hannah doing?" Morgan asked.

"That woman is calm under pressure," JJ said.

"Likely needs that skill to deal with you," Cal said with a wink. "In a good way, of course."

JJ laughed. "Of course."

"How did they explain Meg not being here?" Morgan asked.

"Sassy announced she'd taken ill and had to step away from the show," JJ said. He turned to Morgan. "Meg all squared away?"

"She's not going anywhere." Morgan lowered her voice to a quiet whisper. "I don't understand why she's denying she killed Benny."

"Benny didn't commit suicide?" Cal asked. "When did you find that out?"

"We don't actually know for certain, but it's the theory we're working on," Morgan explained. "His laptop was wiped clean of all fingerprints."

"And it would be hard to imagine someone doing that if it's a suicide," Cal said. "But is it all that surprising Meg would deny any involvement? Why get herself into deeper trouble?"

"It is surprising from the standpoint that she freely admitted to accidentally killing Pierre. Why not go ahead and admit to killing Benny? No, she believed his death was a suicide, as we reported, and she knew nothing else about it."

"You're thinking we have a second killer?" JJ asked. He blew out a breath. "What are the odds?"

"What were the odds of any of the past murders this year happening in this town to begin with?" Morgan said.

"True. You got a vibe yet on who it might be?" JJ asked.

Morgan shook her head. "Not exactly. But I can feel something brewing in the back of my brain."

"Hey Uncle Cal, officers," Henry said loudly as he walked up. Damon shushed him from where he was standing and Henry ducked his head, mouthed *my bad*. "It smells amazing in here," he whispered. "Had a straggler in the shop who couldn't decide between Poe and

Josie Steele. I mean, they're not even close to being the same, other than the Gothic slants. I suggested both."

Cal patted his shoulder. "Good job. I really appreciate your help this weekend. And thanks for selling one of my books."

"Happy to. Looks like they're close to the finale. I was worried I was going to miss it."

"Okay, bakers. Time's up," Damon announced. "Please step away from your displays. Thank you and cut," he said to the camera operators. "You two, Paul and Hannah, please take a thirty-minute break while we tidy things and get set up for the judging," Damon said.

Hannah and Paul hugged, then walked into the cafeteria. Morgan, JJ, Cal, and Henry followed. Elise was waiting on the other side of the door with a tray of fresh vegetables, cheese slices, and crackers and dip. "Thank you, Mom. You and dad have been so good this weekend."

"Sorry we missed the morning bake. How did it go?" She looked around. "And where's Meg?"

"I'll explain everything later, when we have more time," Hannah said. She hugged her mom. "Thanks for being here."

"Oh, please, we're enjoying watching our baby rule the world." Elise glanced at Paul. "No offense. I'm sure you rule in your own way, too." Elise touched Hannah's cheek and went back into the kitchen.

"You do rule in your own way, don't you?" Morgan observed. "Made your money in tech, right?"

"It's not something I really talk about when I'm baking, Captain. But yes, I did."

"A modest millionaire? That's a first," JJ said.

"What are you getting at?" Paul asked, his eyes narrowed.

JJ held up his hands. "Nothing. Just find it interesting someone with as much money as you have would be on a show where the prize is only ten thousand dollars."

"JJ, stop the interrogation now," Hannah said. She huffed and frowned at him. "You have your killer in custody. Let's move on, okay?"

"Hey, JJ," Cal called from the table he and Henry had just commandeered. "Come have a snack with us."

"I don't know you very well," Henry said to JJ, "But you seem a little hangry. Also, love your new ear buds, Paul. Nice ergonomic design."

Paul nodded and went to sit on the other side of the room. Hannah followed him but not before shaking her head at JJ.

Morgan put a hand on JJ's arm. "Come on. Snacks await. Plus, we need to brainstorm about who might be responsible for Benny's death."

They sat down at the table with Cal and Henry. "So where are we?" Cal asked.

Morgan looked pointedly at Henry, then back at Cal.

"Hey, I'm cool. The designer I work for has similar issues with dead bodies turning up when you least expect it." Henry puffed his chest. "And I've helped the local detective solve a case on more than one occasion."

"The apple doesn't fall far from the Joseph family tree, does it?" Morgan quirked a smile.

Cal laughed and noogied his nephew.

Henry ducked away. "Uncle Cal. Respect the hair, please."

"Bakers, it's time to reconvene," Damon called from the doorway.

"We'll talk after," Morgan said to JJ as they followed the bakers into the gym. "I want to bounce some thoughts around about Benny."

Connie stepped into the gym. "Oh, well, look what the cat dragged in once again. Isn't your work done here, Morgan?"

"My work is never done, Connie," Morgan said to the TV reporter/nemesis. "You'd know that if you ever listened to anything I say. What are you up to?"

"We seem to have that one thing in common." Connie sniffed. "I've been invited in for an exclusive sneak peek at the finals. I can't film it. Or write about it until the show airs, so I'm going to start with an interest piece on how baking shows work."

"Fascinating," Henry said. "I've been watching this show since it began, if you'd like a fan's point of view."

Connie looked him up and down, shrugged. "Sure, why not. Let's go sit over there and we can talk after the judging."

"Seems an unlikely alliance," Morgan said as she watched Connie and Henry settle on a bench in the bleachers.

"Trust me. He'll come away with more information than he gives," Cal said, beaming. "I've taught him well."

Damon walked by and said in passing, "Please, no more chatting." He stopped and stood in front of the judging table. "Hannah and Paul. It's now time for you to present your final bakes to Sassy and Bean. A reminder, the winner will not only win ten thousand dollars, but will go on to compete in the national Baker's Dozen Bake-off for a chance to win one hundred thousand dollars."

Sassy and Bean stepped forward. "Thank you, Damon," Sassy said. "Hannah, would you please present your final bake?"

Damon helped Hannah carry the large display of four dozen cupcakes, arranged in the shape of a Ferris wheel with several cupcakes positioned on each seat. "Today, I went back to my great-grandmother's recipe file. She was well known in Bijoux for her beautiful flavors, and she taught me everything I know." Hannah smiled. "The first one is a ginger sponge spiced carrot cake, filled with a light caramel and chopped toasted pecans for crunch, topped with a vanilla French meringue. As you can see, I drizzled caramel and sprinkled the tops with more toasted pecans. I altered the second one slightly. It's a chocolate stout cake with reduced stout wash and espresso buttercream." Hannah smiled. "Grandma used regular beer. I think the stout gives it a richer flavor. And my third cupcake is a blood orange base, milk chocolate Italian buttercream, and sea salt sprinkles."

Bean cut each of the cupcakes in half. "I can see your first cake is well baked, just the right consistency for a carrot cake," Bean said.

Sassy took a bite. "These are most delicious, Hannah. The hint of ginger doesn't overpower the carrot sponge and blends beautifully with the caramel." The two women tasted the remaining cupcakes. "I think your great grandmother would be proud," Sassy said. "Though the blood orange sponge is a tad dry." She wiped her hands on a napkin. "Overall, well done. Paul, would you please step forward?"

Damon removed Hannah's display and then helped Paul with his cupcakes arranged in the shape of a cruise ship. "I was inspired by a cruise I took to Hawaii last year and translated the tropical flavors I experienced into my bakes today. The first cake is coconut, filled with a spiced rum and pineapple jam, topped with mango buttercream and dried pineapple slices. Second is vanilla filled with a passion fruit puree, covered with a hibiscus scented Swiss meringue. And third, is one of my all-time favorites—a banana nut sponge, filled with roasted papaya, and topped with a coconut buttercream."

"Paul, Paul, Paul, Paul, Paul," Sassy said as she tasted a bit of each. "I could eat the entire display, they are that delicious. I find no fault, other than toasting your coconut for the first one would have added to the flavor and given us a little crunch."

"And I'm completely enjoying the rum and pineapple jam," Bean added with a wink.

"Thank you so much," Paul said and returned to his station.

"As you know, bakers, Bean and I will need a little time to deliberate," Sassy said.

Bean leaned toward Sassy and whispered in her ear.

Sassy regarded Bean, then nodded.

"It seems we are already in agreement," Sassy said. "The winner of this final weekend of the Baker's Dozen Bake-Off is...Paul! Well done, Lord Paul!"

Bean clapped her hands together. "Well done, indeed!"

"Thank you." Paul grinned, a hand to his chest. "I'm absolutely thrilled."

"Cheers to you, Lord Paul," Damon said with a smile. "We'll set be setting up in a few minutes to do an interview with you and then give you a rundown on what will be coming next."

"Thanks again, I still can't believe it," Paul said. "Hannah here is so good, I never expected to win. I can't wait to take part in the big show."

"Congratulations," Hannah said as she gave her fellow baker a quick hug. "And I'm stealing one of these." She laughed as she snatched a cupcake from his display.

"I'm so sorry," JJ said as he walked up. He squeezed her hand. "Are you okay?"

"Of course, I am. I just got to compete on a national baking show. This should bring more business to the shop. And I'm happy for Paul," she added with a smile in Paul's direction. "He did an amazing job this weekend."

"Hannah, about your shop," Paul said taking a step closer to her. "Have you thought about expanding Hannah's Heavenly Confections? Selling online? Or franchising?"

"I have but, honestly, the money isn't there to get started. Hopefully in a few years, though."

"I hope you'll consider sooner rather than later, because I'd like to back you."

"Excuse me?" Hannah's jaw dropped.

"Financially. I'd like to invest in your business. As you know, I don't compete for the money. I just love baking. And I've watched you this weekend. You're amazing and I can see how passionate you are about baking too. I'd like to help you grow."

JJ stepped forward. "She doesn't need your money. She's doing just fine."

"JJ," Morgan said out of the corner of her mouth, placing a hand on his upper arm. "How about we go annoy Connie while Paul and Hannah talk?"

JJ shook her off, focused on Hannah. "Hannah, you can't just let this guy waltz in and take over. You don't even know him for crying out loud."

"JJ, how can you say that? You know how much my shop means to me. Paul isn't talking about taking over. He wants to help me build my business." Hannah took a few steps away from JJ. "I—I thought we could talk when this competition was done—and we could make things right again. But now, I don't think that's possible." Hannah's eyes filled with tears. "I don't think I can do this anymore, JJ. I love you but I just can't…."

"Wait. What?" JJ stammered.

Hannah turned to Paul. "I'm sorry about what just happened. I—I would love to talk with you about your amazing proposal."

JJ stood frozen to the spot as he watched Hannah and Paul walk into the cafeteria, then he spun on his heel and stalked out of the gym.

CHAPTER 23

"NO. I WILL NOT HAVE IT!"

Morgan heard Damon shout and rushed out to the main hallway, Cal falling into step beside her. Damon, Sassy, and Bean were huddled off to the side; Sassy's face was red with fury.

"You are completely wrong," Damon insisted. "You need to listen to me."

"What's going on?" Morgan asked.

"Family business," Bean said. "None of your concern."

Morgan decided to reveal what she knew about Benny's death to judge their reactions. "Considering Benny's murder is still unsolved, I'd say everything is my concern."

"What are you talking about?" Sassy asked.

"Benny committed suicide," Damon said. "I was there. I saw him with my own two eyes. End of story."

"But was it *really* a suicide?" Morgan asked. She crossed her arms and considered the trio. Any one of them could have done it, given their past relationships with the dead baker. "It would be easy for any of you to have approached Benny yesterday morning and offer him a cup of coffee on the pretext of talking things through. Perhaps you used cyanide because you knew that's how Pierre died, thought to maybe connect the deaths and get away with murder. So, I ask you again, what were you three arguing about?"

Sassy straightened. "Damon suggested I take a month-long break and rejuvenate after the stress of this weekend." She shot him a nasty look. "He tries to baby me. It's infuriating. *And I will not have it!*"

"Like I said, family business," Bean said.

Morgan ignored her. She was watching Damon. Sassy's words had cut through, deflated him, but she saw a spark of anger underneath the pain and sadness. Maybe she could use that to her advantage. "You really care for Queen Sass, don't you?"

Damon leaned against the glazed block wall and nodded. "I do." He glanced at Sassy. "More than she can recognize or accept, it seems."

"Did you know Benny had written a blog and was going to reveal Meg's cheating? That would have caused quite a scandal," Morgan said.

Cal nodded. "It could potentially do big damage to the Queen's reputation. Maybe even the Duchess's and yours, too, Damon."

"Benny was a slug," Damon said, and Morgan watched as the spark ignited. "A vile, evil little man with nothing better to do than try to take others down." He spat the words out. "He'd been on a tear against Sassy here ever since she broke up with him. That man weaseled his way into this weekend's show, upset everyone but most especially my sweet Sass. As far as I'm concerned, he got exactly what he deserved—" Damon paused suddenly. "I mean—assuming he really didn't kill himself, that is. We only have your word for that, Captain."

"Damon?" Sassy said gently. "Damon, look at me. What are you saying?"

He closed his eyes for a moment and then turned to Sassy. "I had to, Queen. I love you. There. I've said it. I've been in love with you for a long time."

"Oh. Oh, Damon." Sassy's face twisted with sadness. "But I'm old enough to be your—um—much older sister."

"I don't care about your age. And I wasn't going to let that snake Benny ruin you and everything you've worked so hard for."

Sassy wrapped her arms tightly around Damon, tears streaming down her cheeks. "Benny was just an annoying fly," she said in a thick voice. "I wish you had come to me, Damon. I'm so sorry. I should have been paying closer attention. But I promise, I'll be there for you. I promise."

W<small>ITH</small> D<small>AMON LOCKED</small> in the second cell at the station and the paperwork filed, Morgan had only to wait for her Uncle Arnie, the county sheriff, to pick up both Damon and Meg tomorrow and take them to the county jail. She'd made sure they had whatever they needed to get through the night and JJ was going to stay over at the station to keep an eye on things since, as he put it, there was no way in hell he was going to get any sleep tonight anyway. She really felt for him. Break ups were hard. Letting go even harder.

Back home now, Morgan had her own letting go to do.

She walked into her small kitchen, opened the cupboard over the stove, and retrieved the fixings for the perfect s'mores—graham crackers, marshmallows, and super dark chocolate. It was the dark chocolate that made it perfect as the bitterness offset the sweetness of the marshmallow. *Huh. I've been hanging around that baking show way too long.* Morgan had to laugh at herself as she stuffed the items into a backpack along with pretzels and potato chips.

Next, she pulled a soft-sided cooler out from under the sink and added several of her and Ian's favorite Motor City Mustang Stouts along with a bag of ice to keep it all cold.

"You want to come down to the beach with me, Gris? Cal, Liz, and Frankie will be there."

Gris meowed loudly.

"I agree, Cal's a pain. But you do love Frankie. And you'll love Liz once you get to know her a little better. And get past the smell of Beef." She ruffled Gris's head and the cat took off and hid under a chair in the living room. "Guess that's my answer." Morgan shrugged the backpack on and slung the cooler over a shoulder. Before she headed out the door, she picked up a copy of a picture she'd printed out of her and her husband, and tamped down the sadness. *Not tonight.* Tonight, she was all about letting go and focusing on life, not death. She locked the cottage door and headed to the beach. "This evening promises to be epic."

147

DOWN AT THE BEACH, Morgan paused and stood gazing out over the water. The sun had almost set over Lake Michigan, casting a reddish glow in the sky. *Red sky at night, sailor's delight.* She smiled and put her backpack and cooler down on the sand. *Liz, Frankie, and Cal should be here soon.* She began gathering driftwood and placing it in the firepit she'd set up when she first moved to Bijoux. Well, it was more a ring of stacked stones, but it worked well enough.

"Beautiful place you have here."

Morgan froze for an instant, then dropped the armload of wood into the fire pit and turned. "A part of me wondered if you'd eventually show up. The Caribbean not work out for you?"

"You've always had good instincts," James Wheat said. "Barbados wasn't the problem. You had to know I'd eventually have to clean loose ends."

"What loose ends would those be? How about you tell me, just so we're clear?" She sat down on one of the stumps arranged around the pit, motioned to the one across from her. Her heart was racing, head pounding, stomach churning, but she couldn't let him see it. He was a predator and would immediately take advantage. *No, she had to play it cool.* "Have a seat."

"Sure, why not? Just two old friends having a chat, right?" he said with a twist of a smile. He kept his sharp stare trained on Morgan.

"You didn't have to kill Ian, you know. You could have just talked to us." Morgan leaned forward, rested her elbows on her knees, rubbed her ankles. *Damn.* She'd forgotten she'd left her ankle holster in the house. *There was no reason to carry a gun to Ian's memorial.*

"What makes you think I didn't talk to him? Several times, actually." James shook his head. "He wouldn't listen. Ian was so clean, he couldn't imagine doing anything even close to the edge. Things were always black and white for him. Wouldn't even listen to me. I offered to cut him in. Told him I could make him so rich you'd both be able to retire early, enjoy life. If only he'd just gone along with me."

"Ian was a good cop. He was going to report you, wasn't he?"

James snorted a laugh. "He did report me, to Captain Smith. The thing is, she and I were working together so, of course, it didn't go anywhere."

Morgan's heart sank. She'd counted Smitty among her friends, too. Just how deep did the corruption go at the Detroit Police Department? "He didn't quit there, though, did he?" Morgan asked. "I know Ian better than anyone. He was tenacious as hell."

"Yeah, I found out he was going to reach out to Internal Affairs. Couldn't have that. You know what happened next." James stood and stared down at Morgan. "Now, about those loose ends. Where's the evidence?"

Morgan didn't move. "It's been six years. Why wait this long? Why now?"

James heaved a deep sigh. "After Liz talked to Smitty about the informant coming forward, Smitty started monitoring Liz's calls. Look, Smitty is getting ready to retire. She wants this situation put to bed, doesn't want to spend her golden years looking over her shoulder. I get that."

"She's holding Ian's murder over your head, isn't she? Did she threaten to have you extradited? There's no other reason for you to leave the islands that I can see."

"How about you stop stalling, Morgan?" He pulled a gun from his back holster and pointed it at her. "Give me the evidence."

Morgan stood and planted her hands on her hips. "I don't have anything."

James laughed. "Come on. I just told you Smitty was listening in. I know you found something and called Liz." He glanced at his watch. "I also know she's on her way here, so let's go."

Morgan held her ground, not moving. She had to stall for time if she could. "How did it happen?" she asked.

"How do you think? I didn't go there with the intention of killing my best friend and partner of eight years." He rubbed his forehead. "I just wanted to try, one more time, to convince him to go along. Ian told me he'd compiled a case for IA. He reached for his gun, told me he was arresting me. I couldn't let him, I ran at him and toppled him to the ground. We fought over the gun. It flew out of his hands. I managed to get my gun out before he got to his and…I shot him."

Morgan sucked in her breath. The grief and pain punched her in the gut as it had that day, six years ago, when the sheet was pulled back from her husband's dead body. Her ears buzzed and her vision blurred. She took a deep breath, trying to steady herself.

"Hey, Wheat. Wish I could say it was good to see you," Liz said from where she stood on the beach path, about ten feet to his right. "It's not, in case you were wondering." She drew her gun and aimed it at him.

"Not so good to see you either, Shore," James said, keeping his gun trained on Morgan. "Stay where you are, or I'll shoot her."

"Shoot me and you won't get the evidence," Morgan said. Liz moved a half step forward. Morgan saw the motion and glanced at Liz, her eyes held a warning. *Stay where you are.* "I'm the only one who knows where it is."

"Then we don't need her," James said. He swung his gun and, before Liz could react, fired at her, then aimed the gun back at Morgan. Liz crumpled to the ground. "Evidence. Now."

CHAPTER 21

MORGAN HELD her hands up and glanced at her friend. Liz wasn't moving. *She needs help, fast.* Morgan pushed back the fear threatening to overwhelm her. "It's in the cottage. The evidence is there," she rasped out. "But let me help Liz first." Morgan took a step toward Liz. "Please."

"Not going to happen. Keep on walking."

Morgan looked down. Liz was clutching her shoulder, eyes closed, and blood was oozing through her fingers. "I *will* kill you, Wheat, you son of a bitch," Liz ground out.

James aimed his gun at Liz again, pulled back the trigger. "Well, that was a stupid thing to say."

No! Stop! Morgan stepped in front of James but before the gun went off he toppled to the ground. Morgan looked up at and saw Cal standing there, his breath coming in short, sharp gasps, as though he'd been holding it as he snuck up and delivered a blow to the back of James's head.

"Boy, am I glad you have that horrible habit of sneaking up on people." Morgan rasped out a shaky laugh.

Cal shot her an impatient glare.

Regaining her senses Morgan scooped up the gun that had landed a foot away from where James had fallen.

She pointed the gun at her husband's killer, who was groaning and holding the back of his head. "Thank you," she said to Cal.

Cal pulled out his phone. "I'm calling for an ambulance."

Frankie rushed out of the bushes and ran to Liz.

"Where were you?" Morgan asked as she kept the gun pointed at James. "I was afraid you were going to walk into the middle of this."

"There was a car in the driveway we didn't recognize when we got here," Frankie said as she unwrapped the scarf from around her neck. "Ms. Super Heroine here ordered me to stay back at the cottage."

Liz winced as Frankie pressed the scarf against her shoulder. "Ms. Super Heroine? You couldn't come up with something better than that?" Liz tried for a chuckle but it turned into a groan.

"Sorry, how about, 'Ms. Stubborn-Ass?' Is that better?" Frankie sniffed and swiped at the tears in her eyes with one hand as she continued to apply pressure to Liz's wound. "You better not die on me."

Liz cracked a smile. "It'll take a lot more than a bullet to the shoulder to take me out." She reached out to touch Frankie's cheek.

"Cal, there are some zip ties in the front pocket of my backpack," Morgan said, holding the gun steady on James. "Please grab them and bring them to me?"

Cal got the zip ties but instead of handing them to Morgan, he squatted and rolled the semi-conscious James over and securely fastened his hands behind his back.

"How did you know how to do that?" Morgan asked.

"I told you, I've had training."

Morgan pulled out her phone, with shaking hands, and accidentally dropped it. She groaned in frustration.

"It's okay," Cal said in a calming tone. "When I left Frankie behind, she was already calling 9-1-1. I'll text JJ."

"I think he gave me a concussion," James muttered.

"No one here cares." Morgan scowled. "But the paramedics probably will, so I'll let them do their job."

Two hours later, Liz was patched up and James was in a holding cell with JJ standing guard. He would be transferred along with Meg and Damon in the morning. Morgan dropped onto the blanket on the ground by the fire and shook her head. "What an absolute mess this past weekend has been." She glanced at Liz. "And you should have gone to the hospital."

"Please. The bullet clipped the top of my shoulder. The Bijoux paramedics did a good job patching me up. I'm good to go."

Morgan threw her an exasperated look.

"Okay, I'll stop by the hospital in the morning." She held up three fingers. "Scout's promise."

"You know only pinkie swears work here." They locked fingers and grinned.

Frankie leaned gently into Liz's good side and handed her a beer.

"You shouldn't be drinking with painkillers," Morgan said.

"I haven't taken any yet. I wanted to be able to celebrate Ian appropriately."

Cal walked up with an armload of wood and arranged it on top of the now blazing fire. Morgan smiled her thanks and pulled a stout from her cooler, handing it to him. "That was quite a move you did back there."

"*Krav Maga* hammer fist."

"Crazy skills," Liz said.

"So, you were serious when you said you had training?" Morgan asked.

"When am I not serious?" he asked, flexing his arms. Frankie handed him an opener and he popped the top off the glass bottle.

Morgan's stomach flip-flopped. *Not now. Not ready yet.* "Okay, then. Join us in a toast?"

He smiled and sat on the blanket next to her. "I wouldn't miss it."

Morgan held her bottle high. "Ian, I know you're watching, so you know we got the bad guy. I'm sorry I wasn't able to stop James sooner," she said, with a catch in her voice. "Smitty will go down with him once Liz gets back home with the evidence." She wiped at the tears forming in her eyes, then decided to let them flow freely.

Let it go. It's okay... "You were the love of my life and you'll always be in my heart." She picked up the photo of the two of them, then placed it on the fire. Morgan sat back and watched the paper curl and be consumed by the flames. "I promise, from now on, to remember our life together, how you lived, how we lived. Not how you died," she whispered. "And a piece of you will always live on in me." She looked at each of her friends. "Thank you for having my back and sharing this moment with me." She laughed a little. "And for saving my life."

Cal reached out and squeezed her hand.

Morgan caught Frankie and Liz looking pointedly at the gesture and whispering to each other. *To heck with them*, she thought, and squeezed his hand back. "Thanks for being here. For everything," Morgan said softly.

"I'll always be here, as long as you want, Morgan. However you want."

EPILOGUE

"THANKS FOR RUNNING THE TRANSPORT, Uncle Arnie. JJ and I would have had to make multiple trips to the county jail to get these three situated."

"You should have called me, Morgan. Three murder suspects? Three?" He shook his head. "That has to be a busy weekend even by Detroit detective standards."

"She had JJ and me," Liz said. "Your niece is a legit badass."

Arnie laughed. "That she is." He gave Morgan a bear hug. "Always has been."

Morgan, Liz, and JJ waved Arnie off. "Good job, guys. I can't thank you enough," Morgan said.

"I thought everyone could use a coffee and some donuts," Cal said, approaching with a tray of to-go cups and bag of yeast donuts from Dave's Deli. "I would have gotten some of those amazing bear claws from Hannah's, but she's not open today."

JJ came to attention. "Do you know why? That's not like her."

Cal shrugged. "Sign on the window said she was taking the day off to rest after the bake-off. Can't say that I blame her. I could use a day or two off myself."

"Oh, please." Morgan laughed and helped herself to a coffee and donut. "What do you need a day off from? You've barely been at the bookstore for the last few days."

"But the brain is always working," Cal said, tapping the side of his head.

"It looks like you've caught another killer," Connie said as she sauntered up to the station. "You draw them in, then take them down. That's an interesting dynamic."

"What are you inferring?" Morgan asked.

"Nothing more than what I've already talked about. Death seems to follow you." Connie leaned in and said, "And I was right, wasn't I?"

Morgan's eyes narrowed. "About what?"

She leaned back. "The Detroit Killer, of course."

"Connie, how many times do I have to tell you there's no Detroit Killer?"

"What would you call James Wheat, then? He's from Detroit. He killed your husband."

"How do you know about Wheat? We haven't released that information to the public yet," Morgan said. Anger, fueled with suspicion, jumped into overdrive and it was all she could do to keep her expression blank.

"I have a top-notch police scanner, so I hear all the chatter." Connie smiled. "Plus, you're not the only one with friends, Morgan. This is a big county." Connie started dictating into her phone as she walked away.

"What was that all about?" Liz asked.

"That's Morgan's nemesis," Cal said.

"Connie? That was Connie?" Liz mused. "She's prettier than I imagined. I was expecting more of a Wicked-Witch-of-the-West-type vibe."

"She may look like Glinda but she's definitely all Mrs. Gulch," Cal countered.

Morgan laughed. "You called that one."

"I'm going inside to get the paperwork settled," JJ said to Morgan.

"Thanks JJ," Morgan replied, knowing full well her deputy was going to be taking his frustration and hurt about Hannah out on his computer keyboard.

"I see Mayor Ed in the coffee cake line," Morgan said. "I need to update him. Dad, too."

JJ paused at the door. "Would you grab me a piece of cake? Not that I don't appreciate the donut, Cal," he said to his friend. "I'm just going to need cake later to help me get through the day."

Cal nodded. "I understand completely, my friend."

"Happy to," Morgan replied.

Morgan, Cal, and Liz crossed the street to the hardware store where the usual line-up stood waiting to get their coffee cake fix.

"I see you're smiling. Glad you're in such a good mood, Captain," Mayor Ed said to Morgan from the line.

"Uncle Arnie retrieved the three suspects this morning and the baking show is packed up and on its way out of town," Morgan explained.

"You wrapped that all up quickly and with little to no damage to Bijoux's reputation. I commend you for that, Captain Hart." Mayor Ed turned to Cal, regarding him with a dark look. "You, Caleb, are another story."

"Excuse me?"

"The last three events you've been involved in have had murders connected to them. The first murders in Bijoux in almost a hundred years, as you well know." Ed stared hard at Cal. "The town council had an emergency meeting yesterday to discuss events going forward. And, for the time being, you're banned from being involved in any Bijoux events."

"Now wait a minute, you can't make a blanket decision like that without a hearing and a vote," Cal argued.

"It was the executive committee and yes, we can." The line moved and Ed took a couple of steps away from the trio. "It's in the bylaws. The council will handle the planning for next month's Pumpkins and Poe Halloween Festival."

"I've already put it together. Everything's lined up."

"Which we appreciate. Please hand all your notes and contacts over to Tess Clooney. She'll be running the show for the time being." Ed waved as he stepped into Hal's. "Again, good job, Morgan."

"What the hell was that all about?" Liz asked.

"That was a gauntlet," Cal ground out. He clenched and unclenched his hands. "Consider my hat tossed into the mayor ring. I'm definitely running against him."

Morgan touched his arm. "Ed's an ass. We all know that. And we also know there's no way the council can organize an event like you can. Though it would be an interesting way to test the theory that all the murders *are* connected to your festivities…You know, if no one dies next time around."

Cal took a deep breath. "Morgan—."

She waved her hand. "Kidding. Mostly." She smiled. "You might be an okay mayor."

Liz's phone pinged. "It's Beef's sitter. She's had a family emergency and can't feed him this afternoon." She pocketed the phone. "I need to get on the road."

Morgan hugged her friend. "You're the best." She then pulled Ian's micro flash drive, secured in a small evidence bag, out of her shirt pocket and handed it to Liz. "I made a copy, which I've locked away and also backed the data up on my private cloud drive. If you get into any issues, you let me know. If I can help with anything, you let me know. If—"

"I know, I know." Liz took a step back and rolled her eyes. "I'll let you know." She gave Cal a quick hug and said, "Take care of her for me," and headed to her car, where Frankie was waiting to say goodbye.

"Do you think those two will get together?" Cal asked.

Morgan considered his question. "They're still figuring it out, but I think their bond is growing pretty solid."

The coffee cake line moved behind them and caught Morgan's attention. "What say you we get some cake?"

"I suppose it would be a good way to kick off my campaign."

Morgan and Cal excused themselves past the front of the line. Surprisingly, no one chanted *"Cutters, we got cutters"* this time.

"How come you're letting us pass?" Morgan asked Mr. Dominic, who had positioned himself at the door.

"You caught the bad guys. We took a vote and you get a free line pass from now on when you do." He eyed Cal. "But not him."

"Hey, I'm a police consultant now. I helped on the case."

Mr. Dominic gave Cal the once-over, then lowered his cane from where he was blocking the doorway. "Fine. You get a pass too. *This time.*"

Morgan shook her head and laughed.

"It is good to see you happy," Cal said quietly as they entered the hardware store. "I was worried about you."

Morgan stopped and looked up at him. "Honestly, I was too. I slept through the night last night for the first time in I don't know how long. And I owe you a thank you for your help. With everything."

They stared into each other's eyes for a moment. Morgan's heart pounded against her chest and she could feel the heat coming off his body.

"Morgan! Caleb! Come on back! Lemon poppyseed is on the menu today," Able shouted and broke the spell.

Morgan stepped back, smiling, linked her arm with Cal's. "Let's get some cake and talk campaign strategy. I was class president in fourth grade, you know. If you're nice, I'll share my secrets to success."

A NOTE FROM TERI BARNETT

I hope you enjoyed *Cupcakes are Murder*, Bijoux Mystery Series: Book 3.

If you would like to leave a review, which I would greatly appreciate, please visit Amazon.com.

I love to hear from readers! You can contact me through my website at www.teribarnett.com. While you're there, please go ahead and subscribe to my newsletter so you can stay up to date on new releases, special offers, and giveaways.

Now, for a special Halloween treat…keep reading for a Sneak Peek of *Pumpkins Are Murder*, Bijoux Mystery Series: Book 4!

Sneak Peek
PUMPKINS ARE MURDER
Bijoux Mystery Series: Book 4

"You are one ugly pumpkin," Ninja Jeff Malone whispered to the massive, odd-shaped gourd. The master pumpkin carver, who'd earned his nickname for his mad knife skills, was inspecting the crop of pumpkins in the middle of a field. "Nice and big but, beyond that, not at all what I'm looking for." He got down on all fours and foraged through the fog-covered vines, his movements stirring up an earthy smell. "My Spidey-senses tell me the perfect pumpkin is somewhere near here. I just know it is."

The sun was barely up, and the leaves glistened with dew. He'd purposely set out early so he could get a jump on the competition. This year's Pumpkins and Poe Festival was shaping up to be a tough one; all the big names in the biz were in attendance. Sitting back on his haunches he picked up Mr. Ugly again and gave it another once over. Weighing about fifty pounds, it certainly carried a lot of heft, but would it carry the day? Sometimes the ugliest pumpkins turned into the best jack-o-lanterns, depending on the skill and vision of the carver. "Although this one looks like it would be a definite challenge." His gaze strayed across the pumpkin hunting ground stretching out about two acres around him. "Finding the perfect pumpkin will be the key to winning that fifty grand."

"Hey!!! You!!!"

Startled by the shout, Jeff spun on his knees. The weight of the pumpkin caused him to lose his balance and he toppled sideways, hitting the ground hard, his head colliding with what felt like a sharp rock. He blinked a few times to try to clear his vision.

The hooded, black-cloaked figure crouched over him.

"Wha-What the hell?" Jeff sputtered. "Death? N-no way! N-not my time." He struggled to sit up.

The cloaked figure wagged a finger and shoved him back.

Jeff groaned as he fell back, his head smacking the rock again.

The figure glanced around and, pulling out a large pocket-knife, hacked at the thick vine attached to a large pumpkin.

"He-hey, Death, shouldn't you have a better knife than that?" Jeff muttered as he struggled to stay conscious.

Death shrugged as they held the pumpkin in their lap and stabbed the knife into the back of the gourd. Slicing out a large hole, they regarded Ninja Jeff's face. "You know it was convenient, you falling like that and banging your head," the voice rasped from beneath the black hood. "Not what I had originally planned, but all's well that ends well."

Jeff grunted as he tried to roll over and push himself up, but his arms gave out and he landed face down in the dirt. Blood trickled into his eyes from the gash on his head. He lay his hands flat on the ground and, with every ounce of strength he had, managed to roll onto his side. He reached out his hand. "Help me," he pleaded. "Please."

Death brushed a strand of blond hair away from Jeff's eyes and patted his cheek. "I'm sorry. Today's just not your day to win." The figure eased the pumpkin over Jeff's face and began to tug at the vines, pulling the surrounding pumpkins around and over the carver.

Jeff groaned; his voice muffled inside the pumpkin. His eyes blinking through the holes in the jack-o-lantern stared at Death as they tucked their knife back in their pocket and stood. With a final wave, Death turned and strode away.

Jeff screamed as loud as he could, but by now his voice was barely a broken whisper.

"You can fuss and posture all you like, Sinclaire. Nothing you say is going to convince me you're the better pumpkin carver."

Sinclaire Wild ran a hand through her long curly red hair and looked out over the pumpkin patch located just on the outskirts of

Bijoux, Michigan. It was a cool fall morning, still early, but the sun was already bright, carrying the promise of dissipating the swirl of morning ground fog. She and Jimmy Stevens had decided to come an hour early to Gourds Galore and scope things out before the nine a.m. scheduled time for carvers to meet and select their pumpkins for Bijoux's Pumpkins and Poe Festival. She made her way down a row, looking side to side, Jimmy next her. "Why do you have to be such a jerk? I beat you fair and square at the New England Fall Festival."

"You jinxed me."

Sinclaire stopped and stared at her sometimes friend. Well, in truth, Jimmy Stevens was always her friend. They'd even dated for a while. Then the stress of competitive pumpkin carving, and her Siamese cat Hebrides, got between them. "I don't know how many times I have to say it, but I had nothing to do with your favorite knife breaking mid-carve." She harrumphed. "And you can't blame Hebrides for that, either." She lifted the fabric cat carrier slung over her shoulder and whispered to the feline, "Can he, Hebrides?"

Hebrides howled and Sinclaire grinned. "See? He had nothing to do with it."

Jimmy rolled his eyes and frowned. "Bobby Rumble says you're a gremlin."

"And why would you believe anything Bobby says? He just wants to get in your head, so you'll choke this weekend." Bobby Rumble was the self-proclaimed King of Carvers and had an ego the size of three pumpkin fields. With a bad boy attitude to match.

The pair started walking again. Jimmy looked at Sinclaire out of the corner of his eye. "For the record, I think you'd be a cute gremlin."

Sinclaire laughed and swatted him on the arm. A swatch of blue caught her eye. "Hey, what's that over there?" She pointed to a spot a few rows over. "See the blue color? Definitely not natural to pumpkins. Let's take a look." She carefully stepped over the vines, Jimmy following.

"This is really strange. Pumpkins and vines don't grow like this," Sinclaire commented as they approached the tangled mess. "I'm going to guess and say these have been purposely arranged. We should investigate."

Jimmy scoffed. "You watch too many true-crime shows." He leaned past her. "Looks like a scarecrow might have been knocked over. Most likely due to prankster kids or vengeful crows. Only logical explanation."

"You can believe in vengeful crows and that I'm a gremlin, but not that we should take a closer look? Well, I'm going to and if you want to help me shift some of these pumpkins then I would welcome the help. Otherwise, step aside." She squatted and moved a vine and a couple of smaller pumpkins carefully to the side so as not to damage them. "Definitely two denim covered shaped legs. Wait. Jimmy, is that blood on the pumpkin head? Around the bottom edge? And it looks like it's been freshly cut —that edge isn't dried out yet."

He looked over her shoulder and trained his cell phone flashlight where Sinclaire pointed. "Can't be. Pumpkins don't bleed. Neither do scarecrows. Here let me move some of these heavier ones." Jimmy pocketed his phone. He stepped around Sinclaire and bent to shift the large pumpkin. He screamed, stumbled backward, losing his grip on the gourd in the process.

Sinclaire gasped, "Holy Hecate! It's—it's Ninja Jeff!" She scrambled to her feet. "Jimmy, call 911!"

Jimmy whipped out his phone and dialed.

She began pulling at vines and shoving pumpkins away from the unmoving form. She leaned in. "He's not breathing!"

"What's your emergency?" the operator's voice said on speaker.

"I don't know how to explain this, but there's a ninja scarecrow here." Jimmy scrubbed a hand over his face, took a breath. "No. That's not right. Sorry. Not a scarecrow, just a ninja. A dead ninja. In the Gourds Galore pumpkin patch off M22."

I hope you enjoyed this sneak peek of
Pumpkins Are Murder
Bijoux Mystery Series: Book 4

Visit Amazon.com to purchase your copy!

ABOUT THE AUTHOR

Teri Barnett is the author of the Bijoux Mystery Series and the upcoming Lac Voo Mystery Series as well as numerous non-fiction books about Reiki. In a past life, she also wrote historical time-travel / paranormal romance (check out her Oracle Dreams Trilogy).

In addition to writing, Teri is an award-winning artist and nationally recognized commercial interior designer who brings a lifetime of learning and exploration to her writing and workshops. Born and raised in Michigan, Teri currently resides in Indiana where she writes books, does cool art, crochets too many shawls and afghans, and hangs out with Black Cat Lou, her bossy black cat. Though not a Maine Coon, BCL *is* the inspiration for Morgan's rescue cat, Griselda, who makes her debut in Book 2, Mystics are Murder.

When Teri isn't busy working on her next book or redesigning the world, you can find her doing the artist thing in her studio (painting or designing book covers), tromping through the forest, hanging with her kids and grandbabies, or riding through the corn tunnels of Indiana on her motorcycle.

You can visit Teri online at www.teribarnett.com to learn more about her books, contact her, and / or subscribe to her newsletter. Want to follow Lou's antics? You can find her on Insta @TheBlackCatLou.

ALSO BY TERI BARNETT

BIJOUX MYSTERY SERIES

Romance is Murder: Bijoux Mystery Series Book 1

A dead diva, a rotten romance, and a town full of nosy neighbors...

Morgan Hart is home. A former homicide detective in Detroit, Morgan is back in her old hometown of Bijoux, Michigan to take over the reins of Sheriff from her dad, Able. The town has undergone quite a transformation since she lived here with new, kitschy shops along Main Street and a burgeoning tourist trade. Even the iconic pink Firefly Bed & Breakfast has jumped on the bandwagon and is hosting a romance writers' convention with some of the biggest names in the 'happily ever after' biz.

Morgan hopes to ease into her new job, new cottage, and new life – after all, Bijoux hasn't had a murder in a hundred years. But all of Morgan's plans go up in smoke when the biggest diva of the romance world is found dead.

As Morgan and her deputy, JJ Jones, begin their investigation, the townspeople have no qualms about telling her how to do her job, including Caleb Joseph, owner of the local bookstore who is far too nosy (and attractive) for Morgan's comfort.

With a murder to solve and the town in turmoil, Morgan will have to rely on her big city cop skills to catch a killer harboring a hate for happy endings.

Mystics are Murder: Bijoux Mystery Series Book 2

What do you do when your star murder witness only speaks 'Meow?'

Who could predict it would happen again? Morgan Hart didn't expect her first day as police captain of Bijoux, Michigan, the sleepy lakeside town where she grew up, would include a murder, even though that's just what happened. But with the killer behind bars, Morgan can take a breath and start painting her cozy cottage.

Or so she hopes.

When a fortune-telling mystic is found dead at Bijoux's Walk into the Light Psychic Gathering, Morgan and her deputy, JJ Jones, are called in to investigate. The trouble is Morgan's only witness is Griselda, a black cat with blood on her paws.

While every psychic in town claims to know what the cat 'knows,' Morgan relies on her own instincts to sniff out the suspects while dodging her conflicting feelings for local bookshop owner and town hunk, Caleb Joseph. And with her dad, Able's, upcoming wedding to Zoe Buffet, Bijoux's most famous clairvoyant and coffee cake queen, Morgan is under the gun to figure out which mystic is the murderer before the couple says I do.

Cupcakes are Murder: Bijoux Mystery Series Book 3

A cupcake conundrum, a culinary queen on the edge, and a cold-case killer on the loose...

Morgan Hart is settling into her job as police captain of Bijoux, the quaint and quirky tourist town nestled on the Lake Michigan shoreline. Murders have been solved, kittens have been rescued, and progress has been made in the renovation of her cozy cottage by the beach. Despite her grief and ongoing frustration over her husband's unsolved murder six years ago, Morgan hopes an overdue break in the case will finally lead to justice, even if it means exposing a betrayal that could leave her reeling.

Meanwhile, Morgan needs to keep a sharp eye on the upcoming Baker's Dozen Hometown Cupcake Bake-off and TV special hosted by British baking superstar Sassy McComas, aka The Queen of Cupcakes. Rumor has it, Queen Sass is secretly searching for a fresh face to host a new TV show and the competitors vying for the top spot include Bijoux's own pastry princess, Hannah Bellamy.

But when one of the top challengers in the Cupcake Bake-off turns up dead,

Morgan has to sift through the evidence and stop the killer before they strike again and threaten to topple Queen Sass from her throne.

Pumpkins are Murder: Bijoux Mystery Series Book 4

A dead carver, dueling witches, and more tricks than treats...

Bijoux, Michigan is serious about Halloween.

Known as the most haunted town on the Lake Michigan shoreline, Bijoux hosts the annual Pumpkins and Poe Festival—the town's annual homage to Edgar Allan Poe and all things spooky. Pumpkin carvers from around the country flock to Bijoux, slicing and dicing their way into Halloween history. But when one of the carvers turns up dead with a jack-o-lantern on their head and a note with the word Nevermore scrawled in orange ink pinned to their apron, police captain Morgan Hart is called in to investigate.

After solving multiple murders at three previous Bijoux events, the beleaguered police captain steps into the fray once again, along with her down-in-the-dumps deputy, JJ Jones, recently ditched by his girlfriend, local cupcake maven, Hannah Bellamy. Meanwhile, Morgan's own "weak and weary" heart keeps getting tested by Caleb Joseph, owner of the Raven's Nest bookstore. The too-hot-for-his-own-good former Gothic Lit professor has made a hobby out of snooping around Morgan's cases.

It's up to Morgan to thwart various Halloween high-jinks around Bijoux while preventing the town from panicking as she tries to catch a killer who's turned "trick or treat" into the darkest diversion of all—murder.

Mistletoe is Murder: Bijoux Mystery Series Book 5

Skeletons with secrets, prohibition pirates, and holiday hijinks...

Morgan Hart is hoping for a boring Christmas. After eight months of murderous mayhem in her hometown of Bijoux, Michigan, she just wants to snuggle under a warm blanket in front of a cozy fire, with a good book, a hot chocolate (extra marshmallows of course), and Griselda purring beside her. She might even work up the nerve to ask Caleb Joseph over for dinner. Cal, the attractive owner of the Raven's Nest bookstore, has become a good friend since Morgan moved back home to take on the job of police captain.

A bestselling mystery author, Cal recently purchased the old Lawrence Mansion on the edge of town and plans to throw a big Christmas Eve bash. But Morgan's holiday plans—romantic and otherwise—go up in smoke when dark and shadowy secrets are revealed during the clean-up of the 19th century-built home. Can Morgan and Cal uncover the ghostly truth or are they destined for a disastrous deck-the-halls?

ORACLE DREAMS TRILOGY

Historical/Paranormal Time Travel Romance Series

Through the Mists of Time: Book One

London 1865…Valerie Sherwood Brooks has lived her entire life vicariously through books.

Due to a childhood accident, which left her with a permanent limp, Valerie has grown up under the watchful eye of her protective parents. When her banker father announces he's taking the family to Italy to look into an investment opportunity, Valerie is overjoyed at the prospect of leaving London for the excitement of exploring the ancient ruins of Pompeii.

But the romantic young woman who yearns for adventure is unprepared when an earthquake shatters their visit to the old city. Valerie is flung back in time to 79 A.D. where she's thrust into a world of intrigue and danger in the grand home of the darkly handsome, Christos Marcellus. As Valerie tries to keep her wits about her, she is torn between her growing and complicated feelings for Christos and the impending doom of the coming eruption of Vesuvius—knowing it will bring death and destruction.

Shadow Dreams: Book Two

In the village of Paran, in the peaceful plane of Keilah, lurks an evil bent on destruction.

Bethany M'Doro, a Healer and a Knower, possesses the unique ability to see into the past. Her gifts make her invaluable on Paran's archeological digs. The team's most recent discovery—charred bones and a wooden box with an ornate comb—sparks a vision of Eitel, an ancient cult known for stealing souls. Children's souls. A mysterious woman also appears in Bethany's vision, a woman named Elizabeth Jessup, who recently traveled through a portal from the Earth plane.

A widow, Bethany relies on her father to watch over her daughter Sarah, while she is on her expeditions. When Bethany returns home to Paran, her worst fear has come to pass. Sarah is missing along with several other children from the village.

Bethany realizes the resurrected cult of Eitel is responsible for abducting Sarah and the other young ones. And their leader is the traveler, Elizabeth Jessup. Bethany's visions lead her to the Earth plane, to Devil's Gate, Nevada in 1875, to enlist the help of Connor Jessup—Elizabeth's husband—a broken and embittered man.

Bethany now faces the greatest challenges of her life—heal Connor and convince him to travel back with her to Paran to unravel the secrets of Eitel and save Sarah and the other children.

Pagan Fire: Book Three

In the ancient village of Tintagel, Cornwall when old magic still illuminates the night sky, a young warrior embarks on a quest to reclaim his rightful place and the woman who haunts his dreams…

Dylan mac Connall survived the slaughter of his family ten years ago by a traitor to their clan. A young boy at the time, he was rescued by Kate, a wise witch woman who taught him the ways of magic and warned him of the peril that lays ahead if he chooses a path of revenge.

Raised in an abbey by the Sisters of Saint Columba, Maere cu Llwyr is ready to take her full vows and become a nun. But when a handsome warrior named Dylan arrives and claims to be her rightful betrothed, Maere is shocked and afraid of what her future will bring. A wee child when she was abducted from her village, Maere has blocked the memories of that horrific night. She has no recollection of the powerful ancient magic dormant inside her. Or of the childhood friend, who now stands before her, determined, to unlock both Maere's mind and her power.

As Maere and Dylan travel back to Tintagel, they must face the mercurial goddess Morrigu, dangerous Viking raiders, and the evil man who destroyed their families. Can Maere and Dylan survive the battles to come and find their way back home and to each other?

The Oracle Dreams Trilogy is also available as a Boxed Set at amazon.com.

NON-FICTION

Visit ReikiOne.com, PresenceandShadow.com, and/or SacredPriestess Journeys.com for more information.

Beginnings: ReikiOne First Degree Manual

This manual covers the basics of Reiki training and practice, including history, principles, hand positions, and treatment guidelines. Also included is a brief introduction to the chakras and using crystals with Reiki.

The Deeper Journey: ReikiOne Second Degree Manual

The ReikiOne Second Degree Manual includes the three symbols traditionally associated with this degree, explanations and their use, methods of distance healing, sending Reiki through time and space, combining symbols for greater effect, the chakra system, the human aura, and a suggested reading list.

Reiki Master: ReikiOne Third Degree Manual Part A by Teri Barnett, Reiki Master Teacher

This book contains the 4th symbol, its use for Reiki treatments, a discussion of what it means to be a Reiki Master, and how to use crystal grids with Reiki.

Reiki Master Teacher: ReikiOne Third Degree Manual Part B

The Master Teacher Manual contains all the information your students need for stepping into Reiki Master Teacher - A review of the 4th symbol (plus additional data on this symbol), the 5th symbol for attunements, attunement instructions (individual and group), methods and ethics of teaching, getting in touch with your inner teacher, marketing ideas, an extensive reading list, and much more.

The Reiki Teacher's Handbook

A composite of all the ReikiOne Manuals, the Reiki Teacher's Handbook takes your teaching a step further. This book provides you with all the tools you'll need to teach Reiki. Written from the experienced perspective of a master Teacher of the Usui Shiki Ryoho method, you'll find this book adapts easily to other forms of Reiki and can grow with you as you progress on your teaching path.

www.ingramcontent.com/pod-product-compliance
Lightning Source LLC
Chambersburg PA
CBHW020121180626
46812CB00006B/2684